new ventures in recycled fiction / FICTION

NANCY PORTER

Extracted from the novel OLIVER TWIST by Charles Dickens, with an expansion of the story of that doomed woman

Belle Ellis

'Then kill me if you must, for I don't wish to be without you...'

Published by *new ventures in recycled fiction &FictionFaction*
through THE GUTTER PRESS (c) 2016, Belle Ellis

ISBN13; 978-1532825064

Cover by LunaTuna

Palatino Linotype

Printed and bound in Charlottesville, West Virginia, U.S.A.

NANCY PORTER

To understand the story of Nancy Porter, it is necessary to commence with something of the history of Oliver Twist, for it was through her acquaintance with that dear boy that she was to meet her tragic end. He was born in a poor house, and, when he was old enough, was put into the employ of an undertaker; from there he absconded to escape further ill-treatment, and came into the hands of Nat Fagin and his gang of young pick-pockets. Among his new acquaintances were two young women; one named Bet, the other Nancy. There was something about Oliver that appealed to both these women, that caused them to dote on him; but it was in Nancy, especially, that he stirred that aspect of the character of her sex, and of her personally, in that mysterious and inexplicable manner known only to those of the gentler sex.

Nancy Porter is probably of no greater age than twenty years, yet she seems older. Perhaps it is because she was still young - though experienced in a way of life that is far beyond the knowledge of the gentle-folk of that great metropolis of London - that the plight of this boy played, as the expression goes, 'upon the strings of her heart'. Her sense told her, quite reflexively - for she had not considered it - that he should not be recruited into this company of pick-pockets, thieves, coiners, house-breakers and other various vagabonds, villains and law-breakers all, Yet, why it should be that, of all the children who had passed through the tutelage of Mr Nathaniel Fagin, this one should do so, remains among the mysteries of the world; all that may be said of it, is that it is so.

Although he does not feature to any great degree in this account, it is this boy, Oliver, who precipitates the events that are unfolded here. He, quite unaffectedly or with invention or intention, plays upon the emotions of Nancy. Perhaps it is that she sees a part of herself that has been hidden from view, even from herself, since her own childhood. Of this, the author can only speculate, but will refrain from doing so in order to advance the story.

Regardless of his role in these events, of this boy all you need to know is, despite all the rough usage of his childhood, he has remained an innocent. If it were the intent of this extract to delve into the reasons for this it would all be explained, but only at great length. However, it is not the intent of this extract; so it must suffice only to mention that he had inherited this appearance, both physical and in his spirit, or character, from his mother, who, being from a family of gentle-folk, had been unexpectedly and harshly used by the world and its ways before Oliver had been born; indeed a portion of that rough usage had brought *about his birth. She gave her life so that he might live. Having given birth, she died; and it was this event that caused the baby to be placed into the dubious care of the poor-house.*

Although Oliver's mother died alone, there are those who had some dim awareness of his parentage; and wish to discover it, so that the boy may be restored to his inheritance; there are others that wish his origins to remain obscure, so that his inheritance may pass to themselves.

Oliver - having been taken into the streets with Master Bates, known as 'Charly' and Mr Jack Dawkins, known as the Artful Dodger, or Dodger for short, to observe how the arts of the pick-pocket are applied, and to apply them himself - has been arrested. The leader of the gang, Nat Fagin, believes that, since Oliver has not been schooled sufficiently in loyalty to the ranks of the gang, he may give information of the gang's current abode. Fagin's associate, Bill Sikes, who is Nancy's paramour, is, at first, unconcerned. It is Fagin's intention that Oliver, whose innocent appearance he can turn to his criminal intentions and which he considers to be a boon to the fortunes of the gang (but, in the main, to himself) should be restored to his care, if care would be the correct term to apply .

Mr. Sikes, having improved his spirits by swallowing two of three glasses of alcoholic spirit, condescended to take some notice of a conversation, in which the cause and manner of Oliver's capture were detailed; the whole being supplemented with such alterations and improvements on the truth as it appeared to the Dodger to be most advisable to include.

'I'm afraid,' said Fagin, 'that he may say something which will get us into trouble.'

'That's likely,' Sikes observed, with a malicious grin.

'I'm afraid that if the game was up with us, it might be up with a good many more, and that it would come out rather worse for you than it would for me, my dear.'

'Somebody must find out wot's been done at the office,' said Sikes in a low tone.

Fagin nodded assent.

'And if he hasn't peached,' Sikes continued, 'and is committed to trial, then he must be taken care of. You must get hold of him somehow.'

Again Fagin nodded. This much was obvious; but there was one very unfortunate obstacle. This was, that the Dodger, and Charley Bates, and Fagin, and Mr. William Sikes, one and all, entertained a deeply-rooted antipathy to going near a police-office on any ground or pretext whatever. And they all had very good reasons for being so minded. They all sat for a long time and looked at each other, in a state of mournful pondering, when a couple of young ladies made a sudden entrance; one of whom was named Bet, and the other Nancy. They wore a good deal of hair, not very neatly turned up, and were rather untidy about the shoes and stockings. They were not exactly pretty, perhaps; but they had a great deal of colour in their faces, and were hearty. But the feature that probably attracted the attention of their many admirers to the greatest degree was that they were remarkably free and agreeable in their manners. Oliver, when he had first met them had thought them very nice girls indeed. As there is no doubt they were. With their arrival the conversation to flow afresh.

'The very thing!' said Fagin. 'Bet will go; won't you, my dear?'

'Where to?' inquired the young lady.

'To the police-office, my dear,' said Fagin coaxingly.

The young lady said that, while she did not positively affirm that she would not go, but merely expressed an emphatic and earnest desire to be 'blessed if she would'. It was a polite and delicate evasion, which showed that the young lady possessed natural good breeding, one which cannot bear to inflict upon a fellow-creature, the pain of a direct and pointed refusal. So Fagin turned from this young lady, who was gaily attired, in a red gown, green boots, and yellow curl-papers, to the other.

'Nancy, my dear,' said Fagin in a soothing manner, 'what do *you* say?'

'That it won't do; so it's no use a-trying it, Fagin,' replied this particular young woman.

'What do you mean by that?' said Mr. Sikes, looking up at her in a surly manner.

'What I say, Bill,' replied the lady collectedly.

'Why, you're just the very person for it,' reasoned Sikes: 'nobody about here knows anything of you.'

'And as I don't want 'em to, neither,' replied Nancy in the same composed manner, 'it's rather more no than yes with me, Bill.'

'She'll go, Fagin,' said Sikes.

'No, she won't, Fagin,' said Nancy.

'Yes, she will, Fagin,' said Sikes.

And Mr Sikes was right. By dint of alternate threats, promises, and bribes, the lady was prevailed upon to undertake the task. She was not, having recently moved into the neighbourhood of Field Lane (from the remote but genteel suburb of Ratcliffe), under any apprehension of being recognised by any of her numerous acquaintances.

Accordingly, with a clean white apron tied over her gown, and her curl-papers tucked up under a bonnet - both articles being provided from Fagin's inexhaustible stock - Miss Nancy prepared to start out on her errand.

'Stop a minute, my dear,' said Fagin, producing, a little covered basket. 'Carry that too. It looks more respectable.'

'Give her a door-key to carry in her t'other one, Fagin,' said Sikes; 'it looks real and genuine like.'

'Yes, yes, my dear, so it does,' said Fagin, hanging a large street-door key on the forefinger of the young lady's right hand. 'There; very good! Very good indeed, my dear!'

'Oh, my brother! My poor, dear, sweet, innocent little brother!' exclaimed Nancy, bursting into tears, and wringing her hands in a demonstration of a paroxysm of distress. 'What has become of him! Where have they taken him to! Oh, do 'ave pity, and tell me what's been done with the dear boy, gentlemen; do, gentlemen, if you please, gentlemen!'

Having uttered those words in a most lamentable and heart-broken tone: to the immeasurable delight of the entire company of Fagin's pickpockets: Miss Nancy paused, winked, nodded smilingly round, and disappeared.

'Ah, she's a clever girl, my dears,' said Fagin, turning round to his young friends, as if to encourage them to follow the bright example they had just been shown. 'She's an honour to her sex,' Fagin added.

'That she is,' agreed Mr. Sikes, filling his glass, and hitting the table with his enormous fist. 'Here's her health, long life, and wishing they was all like her!'

While these praises were being passed on the skills and crafts of the accomplished Nancy, that young lady made her way to the police-office; being a little naturally timid upon walking through the streets alone and unprotected by the companionable Bill Sikes, as she usually was, she arrived in perfect safety. Entering by the back way, she tapped softly with the key at one of the cell-doors, and listened. There was no sound: so she coughed and listened again. Still there was no reply: so she spoke.

'Nolly, dear?' murmured Nancy in a gentle voice; 'Nolly?'

There was nobody inside but a miserable shoeless criminal, who had been taken for playing the flute, and since the offence against society had been clearly proved, was committed to the House of Correction for one month; with the appropriate and amusing remark that since he had so much breath to spare, it would be more wholesomely expended on the treadmill than upon a flute. He made no answer: being occupied bewailing the loss of the flute, which had been confiscated for the use of the county: so Nancy passed on to the next cell, and knocked there.

'Well!' cried a faint and feeble voice.

'Is there a little boy here?' inquired Nancy, with a ready sob.

'No,' replied the voice; 'God forbid.' This was from a vagrant of sixty-five, who was going to prison for begging, and doing nothing else for his livelihood.

In the next cell was another man, who was going to the same prison for hawking tin saucepans without license; thereby he had been doing something for his living, but was to be jailed anyway, since his trading was in defiance of the Stamp-office.

As neither of these criminals answered to the name of Oliver, or knew anything about him, Nancy made for the bluff officer in the striped waistcoat; and with the most piteous wailings, as she had demonstrated before, demanded her own dear brother.

'I haven't got him, my dear,' said the old man.

'Where is he?' wailed Nancy, in a distracted manner.

'Why, the gentleman's got him,' replied the officer.

'What gentleman! Oh, gracious heavens! What gentleman is it that 'as 'im?' exclaimed Nancy.

The old man informed the deeply affected sister that Oliver had been taken ill in the office, and discharged in consequence of a witness having proved the robbery to have been committed by another boy, who was not in custody; and that the prosecutor himself had carried him away, in an insensible condition, to his own residence, somewhere in the area of Pentonville, the old gentleman there said, having heard that word mentioned to the coachman.

In a state of doubt and uncertainty, the young woman staggered to the gate, and then, having turned the corner into the street, exchanging her faltering walk for a swift run, returned by the complicated route she could think of to the current home of Fagin, the Jew.

'We must know where he is, my dears; he must be found,' said Fagin greatly excited. 'Charley, you do nothing but skulk about, so you'll go out and bring home some news of him! Nancy, my dear, I must have him found. I trust you, my dear, you and the Artful for everything! Stay,' added Fagin, unlocking a drawer with a shaking hand; 'there's money, my dears. I shall shut up this shop to-night. You'll know where to find me! Don't stop here a minute longer. Not an instant, my dears!'

With these words, he pushed them from the room: and carefully double-locked and barred the door behind them. A rap at the door startled him. 'Who's there?' he cried in a shrill tone.

'Me!' replied the voice of the Dodger, through the key-hole.

'What now?' cried the Jew impatiently.

'Is he to be kidnapped as Nancy says?' inquired the Dodger.

'Yes,' replied Fagin, 'wherever she lays hands on him. Find him, find him out, that's all. I shall know what to do next.'

The boy murmured a reply and hurried downstairs after his companions.

'He has not peached so far,' said Fagin. 'If he means to blab us among his new friends, we may stop his mouth yet.'

It was true, Oliver had indeed fainted away and, as a consequence of his condition, he came into the care of the very person whom he was alleged to have committed the crime against, a Mr Brownlow. Having taken ill he remained with this man and was taken care of by a mild old lady named Mrs Bedwin. Once he had fully recovered he was dressed in new clothes and was allowed to venture out into the thoroughfares of the thronging city. But, all the while he had been watched...

Oliver was walking along, thinking how happy and contented he ought to feel when he was startled by a young woman calling out.

'Oh, my dear brother!'

He had hardly looked up to see what the matter was, when he was stopped by having a pair of arms thrown tight round his neck.

'Don't,' cried Oliver, struggling. 'Let go of me. What are you stopping me for?'

The only reply to this, was loud lamentations from the young woman who embraced him; and who had a little basket and a street-door key in her hand.

'Oh my gracious!' said the young woman, 'Oh! Oliver! Oh you are a naughty boy, to make me suffer such distress! Come home, dear, brother, come. Oh, I've found him. Thank gracious goodness heavins!' With this the young woman burst into another fit of crying, and became so dreadfully hysterical that a couple of women there asked a butcher's boy who was also looking on, whether he didn't think he had better run for the doctor. To which, the butcher's boy: who appeared to be of a lounging, not to say indolent disposition: replied, that he thought not.

'Oh, no,' said the young woman, grasping at Oliver's hand; 'I'm better now. Come home directly! Come!'

One of women asked what all this noise was about.

'Oh, ma'am,' replied the young woman, still grasping the child's hand, 'he ran away, near a month ago, from his parents. We are all hard-working and respectable people; he went and joined a set of thieves and bad characters; and almost broke his mother's heart.'

'The young wretch!' said one woman.

'Go home, you little brute,' said the other.

'I am not,' replied Oliver, greatly alarmed. 'I don't know her. I haven't a sister, nor a father and mother either. I'm an orphan.'

'Oh, hear him, how he braves it out!' cried the young woman. 'In such a short time, he has gained such face. He makes out that he doesn't know me.' She drew the shawl off her head.

'Why, it's Nancy!' exclaimed Oliver; and he started back in astonishment.

'You see he knows me!' cried Nancy, appealing to the bystanders. 'Make him come home, or he'll break my heart!'

'What the devil's this?' said a man, bursting out of a beer-shop, with a white dog at his heels; 'young Oliver! Come home to your poor mother, you young dog! Come home directly.'

'I don't belong to them. Help! help!' cried Oliver, struggling in the man's powerful grasp.

'Help!' repeated the man. 'Yes; I'll help you, you rascal! and the man struck him on the head.

'That's right!' cried a looker-on, from a garret-window. 'It'll do him good!'

'That's the only way of bringing him to his senses!' said the two women.

'And he shall have it, too!' the man, administered another blow, and seized Oliver by the collar. 'Come, you young villain! Here, Bull's-eye, mind him, boy!'

Still weak with his recent illness; terrified by the fierce growling of Bulls-eye; stupefied by the blows; and he brutality of the man; and overpowered by the conviction of the bystanders that he really was the little wretch who had run away from his family to be a thief as he was described; what could one poor child do!

It was a low neighbourhood; no help was near; resistance was useless. He was dragged into a labyrinth of narrow courts

What books are these?' asked the man, ' Give 'em here.' With these words, the man tore the volumes from his grasp, and was forced along at a great pace which rendered the few cries he dared to give utterance to quite unintelligible. Even if they had been intelligible, there was nobody to care for them or to respond and give the aid he called out for.

The narrow streets and courts terminated in a large open space. Sikes slackened his pace. Turning to Oliver, he commanded him to take hold of Nancy's hand. Oliver hesitated, and looked round.

'Do you hear?' growled Sikes.

They were in a dark corner, out of the track of passers-by. Oliver saw all too plainly that resistance would be of no avail. He held out his hand, which Nancy clasped tight in hers.

'Give me the other,' said Sikes.

The dog prowled about his owner's legs.

'Here, Bull's-Eye!'

The dog looked up, and growled.

'See here, boy!' said Sikes, putting his other hand to Oliver's throat; 'if he speaks ever so soft a word, hold him!'

The dog growled again; and licking his lips, eyed Oliver as if he would attach himself to his windpipe immediately.

'He's as willing as a Christian, strike me blind if he isn't!' said Sikes, regarding the animal with a grim and ferocious approval.

Bull's-eye wagged his tail; and, giving vent to another growl for the benefit of Oliver, led the way.

It was Smithfield that they were crossing, although it might have been Grosvenor Square, for anything Oliver knew. The night was dark and foggy. The lights in the shops could scarcely struggle through the heavy mist, which thickened and shrouded the streets and houses in gloom; making Oliver's uncertainty the more dismal and depressing.

They had hurried on, when a deep church-bell struck the hour. With its first stroke, Sikes and Nancy stopped and turned their heads in the direction of Newgate.

'Eight o' clock,' said Nancy, when the bell ceased.

'I can hear it, can't I!' replied Sikes.

'I wonder whether *they* can hear it,' said Nancy.

'Of course they can,' replied Sikes. 'It was Bartlemy time when I was shopped. After I was locked up for the night, the row and din outside made the thundering old jail so silent that I could almost have beat my brains out against the iron plates of the door.'

'Poor fellows!' said Nancy. 'Oh, Bill, such fine young chaps!'

'Yes; that's all you women think of,' answered Sikes. 'Fine young chaps! Well, they're as good as dead now, so it don't much matter now, do it, for you or for them.' With this consolation, Sikes appeared to repress a tendency to jealousy, and, clasping Oliver's wrist more firmly, told him to step out again.

'I wouldn't hurry by if it was you that was coming out to be hung the next time eight o'clock struck, Bill,' said the girl, 'I'd walk round and round the place till I dropped, even if the snow was on the ground, and I hadn't a shawl to cover me.'

'And what good would that do?' inquired the unsentimental Sikes.

'I'd want you to know there was someone you knowed, nearby, at such a moment' she said, simply and sincerely.

'Unless you could pitch over a file to me, with twenty yards of good stout rope, you might as well be walking on some road in South America, for all the good it would do for me. Come on, they never wanted a preacher by them while they lived, so they don't need you standing preaching now.'

The girl burst into a laugh; drew her shawl closely round her; and they walked away. 'Still,' she said under her breath, half stooping towards Oliver, and in a reflective tone of voice, 'I've seen a few of them die with a prayer on their lips, even them that never had anything but curses and oaths pass their lips before.'

Oliver felt her hand tremble, and, looking up in her face as they passed a gas-lamp, saw that it had turned a deadly white.

'Don't talk to the boy, unless I can 'ear what you're saying,' commanded Sikes.

They walked all these little-frequented ways for a full half-hour: meeting few people, and those that did appear looked to hold much the same position in society as Mr. Sikes. At length they turned into a filthy narrow street of old-clothes shops; the dog running forward stopped before the door of a shop that was closed and apparently untenanted; it was in a ruinous condition, and on the door was nailed a 'To Let' board: which looked as if it had hung there many years.

'All right,' cried Sikes, glancing about.

Nancy stooped below the shutters, and Oliver heard the sound of a bell. They crossed to the opposite side of the street, and stood for a few moments under a lamp. Sikes held his head down. He heard the sound of a sash window raised; and afterwards the door softly opened. Sikes then seized the boy and, with very little ceremony, all three were quickly inside the house.

The passage was perfectly dark. They waited, while the person who had let them in, chained and barred the door.

'Anybody here?' inquired Sikes.

'No,' replied a voice. The voice which delivered it seemed familiar to Oliver's ears: but it was impossible to distinguish even the form of the speaker in the darkness.

'Let's have a glim,' said Sikes, 'or we shall go breaking our necks.'

'I'll get you one,' replied the voice. In a minute the form of Mr. John Dawkins, otherwise the Artful Dodger, appeared. He bore in his right hand a tallow candle. The young gentleman did not stop to bestow any mark of recognition upon Oliver than a humorous grin; but beckoned the visitors to follow him, they crossed an empty kitchen; and, opening the door were received with a shout of laughter.

'Oh, my wig, my wig!' cried Master Charles Bates, from whose lungs the laughter had come: 'here he is! oh, here he is! Oh, Fagin, look at him! I can't bear it; it is such a jolly game. Hold me, somebody, while I laugh it out.'

With his irrepressible mirth, Master Bates laid himself flat on the floor: and kicked convulsively in an ecstasy of facetious joy. Then jumping to his feet and, advancing to Oliver, viewed him round and round; while Fagin performed a great number of low bows to the bewildered boy. Artful, meantime, who was of a rather saturnine disposition, (he would surely become much like Mr. Sikes, indeed, as he grew) and seldom gave way to merriment when it interfered with business, rifled Oliver's pockets.

'Look at his togs!' said Charley viewing his new jacket. 'Look at his togs! Superfine cloth, and the heavy cut! Oh,! And books, too! Nothing but a gentleman, eh? Fagin!'

'Delighted to see you looking so well, my dear,' said the Jew, bowing with mock humility. 'The Artful shall give you another suit, my dear, for fear you should spoil that. We've been worried about you, young Oliver. Why didn't you write? If you'd let us know you were coming we'd have got something warm, ready for your supper.'

At his, Master Bates roared again: and even the Dodger smiled. The Artful drew a five-pound note at that instant from out of Oliver's jacket pocket.

'Hallo, what's that?' inquired Sikes, stepping forward as the Jew seized the note. 'That's mine, Fagin.'

'No, no, my dear,' said the Jew. 'Mine, Bill, mine. You shall have the books.'

'If you don't make that mine!' said Bill Sikes, putting on his hat with a determined air; 'mine and Nancy's that is; I'll take the boy back straightway.'

Fagin started. Oliver started too, for he hoped that the dispute might really end in his being taken back.

'Come! Hand it over' said Sikes.

'This is hardly fair, Bill; hardly fair, is it, Nancy?' inquired Fagin.

'Fair, or not fair,' retorted Sikes, 'hand it over, I tell you! Do you think Nancy and me has got nothing else to do with our precious time but spend it scouting and kidnapping every young boy as gets grabbed through you? You get all their takings, so give it here, you avaricious old skeleton!'

With this gentle remonstrance, Sikes plucked the note out of Fagin's hand; and looking the old man coolly in the face, folded it, and tied it in his neckerchief.

'That's for our share of the trouble,' said Sikes; 'and not half enough. You may keep the books, if you're fond of reading. If you ain't, sell 'em.'

'They're very pretty,' said Charley Bates grimacing; 'beautiful writing, isn't is, Oliver?' At the sight of the dismayed look with which Oliver regarded his tormentors, Master Bates, who was blessed with a lively sense of the ludicrous, fell into another ecstasy, even more boisterous than the first.

'They belong to the old gentleman,' said Oliver, 'to the good, kind, old gentleman who took me into his house, and had me nursed when I was near dying of the fever. Oh, send back the books and money. Keep me; but pray, send them back. He'll think I stole them; all of them who were so kind to me: will think I stole them!'

'The boy's right,' remarked Fagin, looking round, and knitting his shaggy eyebrows. 'You're right, Oliver, you're right; they *will* think you have stolen 'em. Ha! ha!' chuckled the old Jew, rubbing his hands, 'Quite by accident you have graduated to the status of thief. It couldn't have happened better.'

'Of course it couldn't,' replied Sikes; 'I know'd that, directly I seen him coming through Clerkenwell. It's all right. They're soft-hearted psalm-singers, or they wouldn't have taken him in; they'll ask no questions, for fear that they should be obliged to prosecute, and so get him lagged.'

Oliver looked from one to the other, bewildered, and could scarcely understand; but he jumped suddenly to his feet, when Bill Sikes concluded, and tore wildly from the room: uttering shrieks for help.

Fagin and his two pupils darted out in pursuit, but as Sikes started for the door himself, the girl sprang at the door, and closed it.

'Keep back the dog, Bill!' she cried, 'or he'll tear the boy to pieces.'

Sikes noticed the fire in the girl's eye and called to the dog to stay where it was.

'Let 'im count 'imself lucky if I don't though,' he said as he leaned forward to open the door. Nancy threw herself at him and pinned his arms to his body.

'Leave off me,' cried Sikes. 'It'd serve him right!' he added, as he struggled to disengage himself from the girl's grasp. 'Stand off from me, or I'll split your head open.'

'I don't care for that, Bill, I don't care,' screamed the girl, who continued to struggle violently with the man, 'the child shan't be torn apart by the dog - where you go, it'll follow - unless you kill me first.'

'Shan't he!' said Sikes. 'I'll do that soon enough, if you don't keep off.'

The housebreaker broke free from her grasp and flung the girl away from him to the further end of the room, just as Fagin and the two boys returned, dragging along Oliver.

'What's the matter with her!' said Fagin, looking round at Nancy sprawled across the room.

'The girl's gone mad,,' replied Sikes, savagely.

'No, she hasn't,' said Nancy, pale and breathless from the scuffle; 'no, she hasn't, Fagin; don't you think it.' She got back to her feet.

'Then keep quiet,' said the Jew, with a threatening look.

'I won't do that, neither,' replied Nancy, speaking very loudly. 'What do you think of that?'

Mr Fagin was sufficiently acquainted with the manners and customs of that particular species of humanity to which Nancy belonged to feel tolerably certain that it would be unsafe to prolong conversation with her, at present. To divert the attention of the company, he turned to Oliver.

'So you wanted to get away, my dear?' he said, taking up a jagged and knotted club which lay in a corner of the fireplace; 'eh?'

Oliver made no reply, but looked at the club with fear, his breathing quickened.

'Wanted to get assistance; to call for the police; did you?' sneered Fagin, catching the boy by the arm. 'We'll cure you of that.'

Fagin inflicted a smart blow on Oliver's shoulders with the club; and was raising it for a second, when the girl rushed forward and wrested it from his hand. She flung it into the fire, with such force that it brought the glowing coals whirling and tumbling out into the room.

'I won't stand by Fagin. I won't stand by and see it done,' cried the girl. 'You've got the boy, haven't you? I didn't bring him here to be beaten. Let him be! let him be... or I shall put that mark on you, that would bring me to the gallows.'

With her lips compressed, and her hands clenched, the girl looked at Fagin and then at the other robber: her face quite colourless from the rage into which she had worked herself.

Fagin paused, during which he and Mr Sikes had glanced at one another in a disconcerted manner.

'Why, Nancy!' he started in a soothing tone, 'you... you're more clever than ever to-night. Ha! ha! my dear, you are acting beautifully.'

'Am I!' said the girl. 'Take care I don't overdo it. You will be the worse for it, Fagin, if I do. So I tell you to keep clear of me.'

There is something about a roused woman: especially if she adds to all her other strong passions, the fierce impulses of recklessness and despair; which few men like to provoke. Fagin knew it and saw that it would be hopeless to affect another mistake regarding Miss Nancy's rage; and, shrinking back a few paces, cast a glance, half imploring and half cowardly, at Sikes: as if to hint that he was the fittest person to pursue the case.

Sikes, thus mutely appealed to, and, possibly feeling his personal pride and influence interested in the reduction of Miss Nancy to return to reason; uttered a couple score curses and threats which reflected great credit on the fertility of his invention. As they produced no visible effect, however, he resorted to more tangible arguments.

'What do you mean by this?' asked Sikes; backing up his inquiry with a very common oath concerning the most beautiful of human features: 'what do you mean by it? Do you know who you are, and what you are?'

'Oh, yes, I know all about it. I know, I know,' replied the girl. She shook her head from side to side, with a poor assumption of indifference and laughed hysterically.

'Well, then, keep quiet,' replied Sikes, with a growl like that he always used when addressing his dog, 'or I'll quiet you for a good long time.'

The girl laughed again: with even less composure. She darted a hasty look at Sikes; she turned her face aside, and bit her lip till even blood came.

'You're a nice one,' added Sikes, as he surveyed her with a contemptuous air, 'to take up the humane and gen-teel side now! You'd make a pretty subject for the child to make a friend of. But you'd way lay 'im, you'd kidnap 'im, an' now you get scruples!'

'God Almighty help me!' the girl cried, still in a state of reckless passion; 'and I wish I had been struck dead in the street before I had lent a hand in bringing him here. He's a thief, now! A liar, now! A devil, now! He's all that, from this night forth; isn't that enough for the old wretch, without taking a club to him?'

'Come, come,' said Fagin appealing to him, and motioning towards the boys, who were eagerly attentive to all that passed; 'we must have civil words, Bill; civil words.'

'Civil words!' cried the girl, whose passion had been roused to a frightful pitch. 'Civil words! Yes, you deserve 'em from me. I thieved for you when I was a child not half as old as this!' pointing to Oliver. 'I have been in the same trade, and in the same service, for twelve years since. Don't you know it?'

'Well?,' replied Fagin, with an attempt at pacification; 'and, what if you have, it's your living isn't it!'

'Aye, it is!' returned the girl; not so much speaking as pouring out the words in one continuous and vehement scream. 'It is my living; and the cold, wet, dirty streets are my 'ome.'

'I drove you to the streets? Did I? The streets are where I found you! I gave you a home...'

'And look at how I must pay the rent,' interrupted the young woman. 'Oh, yes, you gave me a home, alright!'

'Still. I gave you a home, didn't I? Who else did? The streets are only your workplace; count yourself lucky because there's some who have the starry sky as their roof, in the middle of winter too,' Fagin hissed at her.

'Oh, yes! I'm the lucky one, with the streets as my workplace; you're the wretch that drove me to them, and that'll keep me there, day and night, night and day, till I die!' Nancy raved back at him.

'I shall do you a mischief!' interposed Sikes, not so much on behalf of Fagin, somuch as he was tired with her raving.

'And you'd be right to,' added Fagin, goaded by these reproaches; 'if you say anything else!'

The girl said nothing more; but, tearing at her hair and dress in a transport of passion, made such a rush at him as would probably have left the marks of her revenge upon him, had not her wrists been seized by Sikes at the moment she would strike; upon which, she made a few ineffectual struggles against his overpowering might. Sikes felt her struggles weakening and let go of one of her wrists and raised his arm to strike her, but, before he could do so, she fainted away.

'She's all right now,' said Sikes, picking up her small form and laying her in a chair. 'She's uncommonly strong in the arms, when she's worked up in this way.'

Fagin wiped his forehead: and smiled, as if it were a relief to have the disturbance over. For many observers, if they had been there to witness it, Nancy's outburst would have seemed extraordinary, but neither he, nor Sikes, nor the boy pick-pockets, seemed to consider it in any other light than a common enough occurrence which was incidental to their business.

'It's the worst of having to do with women,' said Fagin, replacing his club; 'but they're clever, and 'ave other uses, so as we can't get on, in our line, without 'em. You know what they're like, Bill, a woman gets sentimental over a boy when he's around the age Oliver is; they see's something in them, but it never survives, I don't know what it is. I've seen it so many times even among... no, especially, among the women in our line. Never mind, when 'e gets a couple of years older she'll lose interest. So don't bother about it,' concluded Fagin.

'And then she'll move onto the next pathetic wretched recruit you bring in,' Sikes suggested.

'Maybe,' Fagin said, 'That's as maybe. Still it's only the first time that Nancy's been like this. Be light in the hand in how you treat her when you get her 'ome, Bill. Won't you?'

Several days passed before Fagin and Nancy met again; but Nancy, regardless of everything that had passed on that other evening, had made her way home with Bill Sikes as she always did.

The dog growled at the merest sound of the handle of the room-door being touched.

'Only me, Bill; only me, my dear,' said Fagin looking in.

'Come on in then,' said Sikes.

The dog leapt to it's feet and growled at the incomer. 'Lie down, you old brute!' hissed Sikes at the dog, 'Don't you know the devil when he's got a great-coat on?'

Apparently, the dog had been deceived by Fagin's outer garment; for as he unbuttoned it, and threw it over the back of a chair, he retired to the corner from which he had risen: wagging his tail as he went, to show that he was as well satisfied as it was in his nature to be.

'Well!' said Sikes.

'Well, my dear,' replied Fagin. 'Ah! Nancy.'

This was uttered with just enough embarrassment to imply a doubt of its reception; for Fagin and the young woman had not met since she had interceded on Oliver's behalf. All doubts upon the subject, if he had any, were removed by the young lady's behaviour. She took her feet off the fender, pushed back her chair, and bade Fagin to draw up a chair, without saying more about it. She was resting her head on one hand, or she held the side of her head, either for it's soreness, or to hide a mark there.

He glanced sidelong at her as he sat down, and noted the fresh bruises that he knew Sikes had brought upon her, as a corrective admonishment for her last outburst, and that were always administered when Nancy rebelled.

'It is cold, Nancy dear,' said Fagin, as he warmed his skinny hands over the fire. 'It seems to go right through one,' added the old man.

'It must be a piercer, if it finds its way through your heart,' said Sikes. 'Give him something to drink, Nancy. Make haste! It's enough to turn a man ill, to see his lean old carcass shivering in that way, like an twisted ghost just rose from the grave.'

Fagin looked at Sikes as she turned away, and mouthed as much as whispered, referring to the bruises, approvingly, 'Just enough, Bill. But not too much. Not too much as to bring you to the gallows.'

Nancy brought a bottle from a cupboard, in which there were many others. Sikes poured out a glass of brandy, and bade Fagin to drink it.

'Quite enough, quite, thanks Bill,' replied the Jew, putting down the glass after just setting it to his lips.

'What! You're afraid of our getting the better of you, are you?' inquired Sikes, fixing his eyes on him. With a hoarse grunt of contempt, Sikes seized the glass, and threw the remainder of its contents into the ashes: as a preparation to filling it again for himself: which he did at once.

Fagin glanced round the room, as his companion tossed down the second glassful; not in curiosity, for he had seen it often before; but in a restless and suspicious manner which was his habit. It was a meanly furnished apartment, with nothing but the contents of the closet to indicate that its occupier was anything but a working man; and with no more suspicious articles displayed than two heavy bludgeons which stood in a corner, and a 'life-preserver' that hung over the chimney-piece.

'There,' said Sikes, smacking his lips. 'Now I'm ready.'

'For business?' inquired the Jew.

'For business,' replied Sikes; 'so say what you've got to say.'

'About the crib at Chertsey, Bill?' said the Jew, drawing his chair forward, and speaking in a very low voice.

'Yeah. Wot about it?' inquired Sikes.

'Ah! you know what I mean, my dear,' Fagin said. 'He knows what I mean, Nancy; don't he?'

'No, he don't,' sneered Mr. Sikes. 'So speak out, and call things by their right names; don't sit there, winking and blinking, and talking to me in hints. Wot d'ye mean?'

'Hush, Bill, hush!' said Fagin, 'somebody will hear us, my dear.'

'Let 'em hear!' said Sikes; 'I don't care.' But as Sikes DID care, on reflection, he dropped his voice, and grew calmer.

'There, there,' said Fagin, coaxingly. 'It was only my caution, nothing more. Now, my dear, when is it to be done, Bill, eh? Such plate, my dear!' he said: rubbing his hands.

'Not at all,' replied Sikes coldly.

'Not to be done at all!' echoed Fagin, leaning back in his chair.

'No, not at all,' rejoined Sikes. 'At least it can't be a put-up job, as we expected.'

Along silence ensued; during which the Jew was plunged in deep thought with his face wrinkled into an expression of perfectly demoniacal villainy. Sikes eyed him from time to time. Nancy, fearful of irritating the housebreaker, sat with her eyes fixed upon the fire, as if she had been deaf to all that passed; as indeed she partially was, although she did not yet know it. For the present she experienced the sensation as a ringing in the head and a slight dizziness that persisted; the last beating that Sikes had administered had damaged her hearing on one side, the side of the head that she had taken to holding a hand to.

'Fagin,' said Sikes, abruptly breaking the stillness; 'is it worth fifty shiners extra, if it's safely done from the outside?'

'Yes,' said the Jew, suddenly rousing himself.

'Is it a bargain?' inquired Sikes.

'Yes, my dear, yes,' replied Fagin; his eyes glistening, and every muscle in his face working, with the excitement that the inquiry awakened.

'Then let it come off as soon as you like. Me and Toby were over the garden-wall the night afore last, sounding the panels of the door and shutters. The crib's barred up at night like a jail; but there's one part we can crack, safe and softly.'

'Which is that, Bill?' asked Fagin eagerly.

'Why,' whispered Sikes, 'as you cross the lawn....' Sikes stopped short, as the girl, scarcely moving her head, looked suddenly round, and pointed for an instant to the Jew's face. 'Never mind which part it is. You can't do it without me, I know; but it's best to be on the safe side when one deals with you.'

'As you like it, my dear, as you like' replied Fagin. 'Is there no help wanted?'

'A centre-bit and a boy,' said Sikes. 'The first we've both got; the second you must find.'

'A boy!' exclaimed the Jew. 'Oh! then it's a panel, eh?'

'Never mind wot it is!' replied Sikes. 'I want a boy! If I'd only got that young boy of Ned, the chimney-sweeper's! He kept him small on purpose, and hired him out by the job. But the father got lagged; and the Juvenile Delinquent Society cames for the young 'un, and takes 'im away from a trade where he was earning, teaches him to read and write, and in time makes a 'prentice of him,' said Sikes, his wrath rising with the recollection of this grievous wrong, 'and so it is that they go on. If they'd got money enough we shouldn't have half a dozen boys left in the whole trade, in a year or two.'

'We wouldn't,' acquiesced the Jew, who had been considering during this speech, and had only caught the last sentence. 'Bill!'

'What?' inquired Sikes.

Fagin nodded towards Nancy, who was still gazing at the fire, rubbing the side of her head; he intimated, by a sign, that he would have her told to leave the room. Sikes shrugged his shoulders, thinking that the precaution was unnecessary; but complied, nevertheless. He requested that Miss Nancy fetch him a jug of beer.

'You don't want beer,' said Nancy, folding her arms and retaining her seat.

'I tell you I do!' replied Sikes.

'Nonsense,' rejoined the girl coolly, 'Go on, Fagin. I know what he's going to say, Bill; he needn't mind me.'

Fagin still hesitated. Sikes looked from one to the other.

'You don't mind the old girl, do you, Fagin?' he asked. 'You've known her long enough to trust her. She ain't one to blab, are you Nancy?'

'I should think not!' she replied: drawing her chair up to the table, and putting her elbows upon it.

'No, no, my dear, I know you're not,' said the Jew; 'bu...' and again the old man paused.

'But wot?' inquired Sikes.

'I didn't know whether she mightn't p'r'aps be out of sorts, you know, as she was the other night,' he replied.

At this, Nancy burst into a loud laugh; and, swallowing a glass of brandy, shook her head with an air of defiance, and burst into exclamations of 'Keep the game a-going!' 'Never say die!' and the like. These seemed to have the effect of re-assuring both; for Fagin nodded his head with a satisfied air, and resumed his seat: as did Sikes likewise.

'Now, Fagin,' said Nancy with a laugh. 'Tell Bill about Oliver!'

'Ha! you're a clever one, my dear: the sharpest of girls!' said Fagin, patting her on the neck. 'It *was* about Oliver I was going to speak, sure enough.'

'What about him?' demanded Sikes.

'He's the boy for you,' replied the Jew in a hoarse whisper; laying his finger on the side of his nose, and grinning frightfully.

'He!' exclaimed. Sikes.

'Have him, Bill!' said Nancy. 'I would, if I was in your place. He mayn't be so much up, as any of the others; he's not trained up yet, but that's not what you want, he's only to open a door for you. Bill.'

'He's been in good training these last few weeks, and it's time he began to work for his bread. Besides, the others are all too big.' added Fagin.

'Well, he is just the size I want,' said Sikes, ruminating.

'And will do everything you want, my dear,' interposed the Jew; 'He can't help himself, if you frighten him enough.'

'Frighten him!' echoed Sikes. 'It'll be no sham frightening him, mind. If there's anything queer about him when we once get into the work. You won't see him alive again, Fagin. Think of that, before you send him. Mark my words! In for a penny, in for a pound.' said the robber, poising a crowbar, which he had drawn from under the bedstead.

'I've thought of it all,' said Fagin with energy. 'I've - I've had my eye upon him, my dears. Once let him feel that he is one of us; fill his mind with the idea that he has been a thief; and he's ours! Ours for life. Oh-o! It couldn't have come about better! The old man crossed his arms upon his breast; and, drawing his head and shoulders in, literally hugged himself for joy.

'Ours!' said Sikes. 'Yours, you mean.'

'Perhaps I do,' said Fagin, with a shrill chuckle. 'Mine, if you like, Bill. But, it's like you said about Ned's young 'un, Oliver could be hired out by the job too; but you can have him "gratis", seeing as he's still an apprentice, learning the trade, like.'

'And wot,' said Sikes, scowling, 'wot makes you take so much pains about one chalk-faced kid, when you know there are fifty boys snoozing about Common Garden every night, as you might pick from?'

'Because they're of no use to me, my dear,' Fagin replied, 'not worth it. Their looks convict 'em when they get into trouble, and I lose 'em all. With this boy, properly managed, I could do what I couldn't with twenty of 'em. Besides,' Fagin continued, 'he has us now so he must be in the same boat with us. Never mind how he came there; it's quite enough for my power over him that he was in a robbery; that's all I want. Now, how much better this is, than being obliged to put the boy out of the way - which would be dangerous, and we should lose by it.'

As Sikes was about to express disgust at Fagin's affectation of humanity. Nancy asked 'When is it to be done?'

'Ah, to be sure, when is it to be done, Bill?'

'The night arter to-morrow,' replied Sikes in a surly voice.

'Good,' said the Jew; 'there's no moon. And it's all arranged about bringing off the swag, is it?'

Sikes nodded.

'And about....'

'Oh, it's all planned,' replied Sikes, interrupting him. 'Never mind the particulars. You'd better bring the boy to-morrow night. I shall get off an hour arter daybreak. Then you hold your tongue, and keep the melting-pot ready, and that's all you'll have to do.'

It was decided that Nancy should journey to Fagin's next evening when night had set in, and bring Oliver away with her; it was also arranged that Oliver should pass into the care and custody of Mr William Sikes; and further, Fagin said that Sikes should deal with him as he thought it fit; and should not be held responsible by him for any mischance or evil that might be necessary to visit on him. It was understood that this compact was binding; any representations made by Mr Sikes on his return should be required to be confirmed and corroborated by the testimony of flash Toby Crackit.

These affairs being settled, Sikes proceeded to drink brandy at a furious rate, and to flourish the crowbar in an alarming manner; yelling most unmusical snatches of song, until, in a fit of professional enthusiasm, he insisted upon producing his box of housebreaking tools: having got them from a hidden place in the upper part of the building he had no sooner stumbled in with them and opened for the purpose of explaining the nature and properties of the various implements, and the peculiar beauties of their construction, than he fell over the box upon the floor, and went to sleep where he fell.

'Good-night, Nancy,' said Fagin, muffling himself up as before.

'Good-night.'

Their eyes met, and Fagin scrutinised her, narrowly. There was no flinching about the girl. She was as true and earnest in the matter as any lawbreaker could be. Fagin again bade her good-night, and, bestowing a sly kick upon the prostrate form upon the floor while her back was turned, groped his way in darkness down the stairs.

'Always the way!' muttered Fagin to himself. 'These women, no matter that they be of the worst sort, there is still a very little thing that serves to call up some long-forgotten feeling; and, the best of it is that it never lasts!'

Beguiling the time with these pleasant reflections, Fagin wended his way, through mud and mire, to his gloomy place: where the Dodger was sitting up, impatiently awaiting his return.

On the following evening, as Oliver had concluded his prayer but remained with his head buried in his hands, there was a rustling noise that roused him.

'Who's that!' he said as he started up, and caught sight of a figure standing by the door.

'Me. Only me,' replied a tremulous voice.

Oliver raised the candle: it was Nancy, come to fetch him, just as the conspiring trio had arranged.

'Put down the light,' said the girl, turning away her head. 'It hurts my eyes.'

Oliver saw a teary glint in her eye, and that she was very pale, and inquired if she were ill. The girl made a brave attempt at a smile but barely succeeded. She shivered, or more correctly she seemed to shake and rock upon her feet, and threw herself into a chair, with her back towards him: but made no other response.

'Has anything happened?' asked Oliver. 'Can I help you? I will if I can. I will, indeed.'

She glanced round at him. 'I know you would,' she observed, and added under her breath, 'That's the worst of it.' She sat and rocked herself to-and-fro; and, uttering a gurgling sound, she gasped for breath.

'Nancy!' cried Oliver, 'What is it?'

The girl beat her hands upon her knees; and, suddenly stopping, drew her shawl close round her: and shivered with cold. Oliver stirred the fire. Drawing her chair close by it, she embraced the boy and sat for a while, without speaking; til she seemed to recollect where she was and raised her head, and looked at him for a moment.

'I don't know what it is that comes over me sometimes,' she said, affecting to busy herself in arranging her dress; 'it's this damp dirty room, I think. All the damp, and all the dirt, it affects me somehow, yet I ought to be used to it. I've never known anything else, still.... Now, now dear,

Mr Fagin told you that you are to come way with me, yes? Are you ready? I have come from Bill,' said the girl.

'What for?' asked Oliver, recoiling.

'What for?' echoed the girl, raising her eyes, and averting them the moment they encountered the boy's face. 'Oh! For no harm.'

'I don't believe it,' said Oliver: who had watched her closely.

'Have it your own way,' replied the girl, affecting to laugh. 'For no good purpose, then. For you'll not be serving angels, that's certain.'

Oliver could see that he had some power over the girl's better feelings, and thought of appealing to her compassion. But, then, the thought darted across his mind that it was barely eleven o'clock; and that many people were still in the streets: of whom surely some might be found to give credence to his tale. As the reflection occurred to him, he stepped forward: and said that he was ready. His brief consideration was not lost on Nancy. She eyed him narrowly and cast a look upon him which sufficiently showed that she guessed what had been passing in his thoughts.

'Hush!' said the girl, stooping over him. 'You can't help yourself. I have tried hard for you, but it's all to no purpose. You are hedged round. If ever you are to get loose from here, this is not the time.'

Struck by her manner, Oliver looked up in her face with surprise. Her face was white and her expression agitated; and she trembled with the earnestness of what she had said. Her expression seemed to carry greater import and weight, for her, than the mere words themselves. She seemed to speak the truth.

'I have saved you from being ill-used once, by his damned dog, and I will again if needs be,' continued the girl. 'I have promised that you will be quiet; if you are not, you will only do harm to yourself and to me,' she halted, 'and perhaps be my death. See here! I have borne all this for you already.'

She pointed to livid bruises on her neck and arms; and said: 'Remember this! These I have got for you. Don't let me suffer more. I accept these, for they belong to me, such as I am. If I could help you, I would; but I have not the power. They don't mean to harm you; and whatever they make you do, remember, it is no fault of yours. But hush! You must be quiet and not argue when you get there, for every word from you there will be a blow for me later. And my head is sore, and I can hardly hear in one ear,' she added patting the right side of her head. Give me your hand. Make haste! Your hand!'

Oliver instinctively placed his hand in hers, as he had done, much more gladly, with the old nurse, at Mr Brownlow's. Blowing out the light, she drew him after her up the stairs. The door was opened, quickly, by someone shrouded in the darkness, and was as quickly closed when they had passed out. A hackney-cabriolet was waiting; the girl pulled him in with her, and drew the curtains closed. The driver wanted no directions, but lashed his horse into full speed, without any delay.

The girl still held Oliver fast by the hand. She rubbed the side of her head as she continued to pour into his ear, further assurances and warnings. All was so quick and hurried, that he had scarcely time to recollect where he was when the carriage stopped at a house.

For a brief moment, Oliver cast a hurried glance along the empty street, and a cry for help hung upon his lips. But the girl's voice was in his ear, beseeching him to remember how she would also suffer, that he had not the heart to utter it. While he hesitated, the opportunity was gone; he was already in the house, and the door was shut.

'This way,' said the girl, releasing her hold for the first time. 'Bill!'

'Hallo!' replied Sikes: appearing at the head of the stairs, with a candle. 'Come on!'

This was an uncommonly hearty welcome, from a person of Mr Sikes' temperament. Nancy, appearing much gratified by the tone, saluted him cordially.

So you've got the kid,' observed Sikes, as he lighted them up the stairs.

'Here he is,' replied Nancy.

'I aren't taking Bull's-eye,' he added as some sort of reassurance, or concession, to the girl, as they reached the room: and he closed the door as he spoke. 'He'd 'ave been in the way.

'Good,' the girl said simply, and she gave a half-smile towards Oliver while Bill Sikes back was turned away from them.

'Did he come quiet?' inquired Sikes.

'Like a lamb,' replied Nancy.

'I'm glad to hear it,' said Sikes, looking grimly at Oliver; 'for the sake of his young carcass, as much as yours: as he would otherways have suffered for it. Come here, young 'un; and let me read you a lecture, which is as well got over at once.'

Addressing his pupil, Sikes pulled off Oliver's cap and threw it into a corner; and then, taking him by the shoulder, sat himself by the table, and stood the boy in front of him.

'Now, first: do you know wot this is?' inquired Sikes, taking up a pocket-pistol which lay on the table.

Oliver nodded that he did.

'Well, then, look here,' continued Sikes. 'This is powder; that 'ere's a bullet; and this is a little bit of a old hat for waddin'.'

Oliver murmured his comprehension; and Mr. Sikes proceeded to load the pistol, with deliberation.

'Now it's loaded,' said Mr. Sikes, when he had finished.

'Yes, I see it is, sir,' replied Oliver.

'Well,' said the robber, grasping Oliver's wrist, and pushing the barrel to his temple; at which moment the boy could not repress a start, and Nancy turned away from looking; 'if you speak a word when you're out o'doors with me, except when I speak to you, that bullet will be in your head without further notice. So, if you do make up your mind to speak without leave, say your prayers first.'

Having bestowed a scowl upon the object of his warning, to increase its effect, Sikes put down the pistol and continued. 'As near as I know, there isn't anybody as would be asking very partickler arter you, if you was disposed of; so I needn't take this devil-and-all of trouble to explain matters to you, if it warn't for your own good. D'ye hear me?'

'The short and the long of what you mean,' said Nancy, turning back to face them, speaking very emphatically and frowning at Oliver as if to indicate that he must give his serious attention to her words, but all the while reiterating Bill Sikes words and intent: 'is, that if you're crossed by him in this job, you'll prevent his ever telling tales by shooting him through the head, and will take your chance of swinging for it, as you do for a great many other things in the way of business, every month of your life.'

'That's it!' observed Mr. Sikes, approvingly; 'there's something about women, they can always put things in the fewest words. Except when they're blowing up; and then they lengthens it all out. And now that he knows, let's have some supper, and get a snooze before starting.'

Nancy quickly laid the cloth; disappearing for a few minutes, she returned with a pot of porter and a dish of sheep's heads. The worthy gentleman, perhaps stimulated by the prospect of being out on active service, was in great spirits; in proof of it he drank all the beer at a draught, and was in such a good-humour that he did not utter more than four-score oaths during the whole of the meal.

Supper being ended - Oliver had no great appetite for it - Sikes disposed of a couple of glasses of spirits and water, and threw himself on the bed; ordering Nancy to call him at five precisely. Oliver stretched himself in his clothes, by command of the man, on a mattress upon the floor; and the girl, mending the fire, sat before it, in readiness to rouse them at the appointed time. For a long time Oliver lay awake, thinking it not impossible that Nancy might seek an opportunity of whispering some further advice; but the girl sat brooding over the fire, resting her head all the while on the one hand, without moving, save now and then to trim the light. Weary with watching her and from his great anxiety, he fell asleep.

When he awoke, the table was covered with tea-things, and Nancy was busily engaged in preparing breakfast. Sikes, meanwhile, was thrusting various articles into the pockets of his great-coat which hung over the back of a chair. It was not yet daylight; for the candle was still burning, and it was dark outside.

'Now, then!' growled Sikes, as Oliver started up; 'half-past five! Look sharp, for it's late as it is.'

Nancy, scarcely looking at the boy, threw him a handkerchief to tie round his throat; Sikes gave him a large rough cape to button over his shoulders. He gave his hand to the robber, who, merely pausing to show him, with a menacing gesture, that he had the pistol in a side-pocket of his great-coat, clasped it firmly in his, and, exchanging a farewell with Nancy, led him away.

Oliver turned, for an instant, when they reached the door, in the hope of meeting a look from the girl. But she had resumed her old seat in front of the fire, and sat, perfectly motionless before it.

This venture, 'the crack' as it is known to these professional gentlemen, failed. The whole neighbourhood was roused and, in the course of the pursuit, several shots were fired. By one of these shots, Oliver was hit, and was badly injured. He lay unconscious in a field for more than a day.

The following morning he who had discharged the firearm was worried that he might have been responsible for the killing, or for grievously wounding, a fellow creature, while a companion continued to fret that the house-breakers had arrived so unexpectedly and in the silence of the night too.

The shooting of Oliver Twist, curiously enough, worked to improve his fortunes, for through the incident he passed, once more, out from the company of the pick-pockets and thieves, and into the care of a charitable persoon; she was a lovely young woman, named Miss Rose Maylie. The doctor, called to attend to the boy, on hearing that those that had armed themselves and shot the boy, were especially troubled about the robbery being attempted in the night-time and that it had happened so unexpectedly, pondered the likelihood of it being the custom of gentlemen in the housebreaking way to transact business at noon, and to make an appointment, by post, a day or two previous, so as to establish, for the convenience of the housekeeper, the time their house ought to be broken open and ransacked.

It is here that another character, Monks, enters the story. He is the person alluded to at the commencement; he who wishes that the true ancestry of Oliver Twist be kept obscure, that it may work to his own advantage. While it is not necessary to commit ourselves to his story, his entry precipitates the events that affect Nancy to the highest degree, so he must be alluded to.

Fagin's face wore an expression of anxiety and thought. He called a hack-cabriolet, and bade the man drive to Bethnal Green. He dismissed him within a quarter of a mile of Sikes's residence, and walked the remaining distance.

'Now,' he muttered, as he knocked at the door, 'if there is any deep play here, I shall have it out, my girl, cunning as you are.'

Fagin crept softly upstairs, and entered without knocking. The girl was alone; lying with her head upon the table, and her hair straggling over it.

'She's been drinking,' thought Fagin, 'or perhaps she is only miserable.'

The old man turned to close the door, and the noise roused the girl. He recited Toby Crackit's story and she eyed his crafty face narrowly, as he did so. When it was concluded, she sank into her former attitude, and did not speak. She changed her position once or twice and shuffled her feet upon the ground. During the silence, Fagin looked restlessly about the room, as if to assure himself that there were no appearance of Sikes having covertly returned. Apparently satisfied, he made an effort to open a conversation; but the girl heeded him no more than if he were the table top. He made another attempt; and rubbing his hands together, said, in his most conciliatory tone, 'And where should you think Bill was now, my dear?'

The girl moaned out some half intelligible reply, that she could not tell; and seemed, from the smothered noise that escaped her, to be crying.

'And the boy, too,' said Fagin, straining his eyes to catch a glimpse of her face. 'That poor leetle child! Left in a ditch, Nance; only think!'

'The child,' said the girl, suddenly looking up, 'is better where he is, than among us; and if no harm comes to Bill from it, I hope he lies dead in the ditch.'

'What!' cried the Jew, in amazement.

'I do,' replied the girl, meeting his gaze. 'I shall be glad to have him away from my eyes, and to know that the worst is over. I can't bear to have him around here. The sight of him turns me against myself, and all of you.'

'Pooh!' said Fagin, scornfully. 'You're drunk.'

'Am I?' the girl said bitterly. 'You'd never have me anything else, if you had your will, except; the humour doesn't suit you, does it?'

'No!' returned Fagin. 'It does not.'

'Change it, then!' responded the girl, with a laugh.

fingers. If he comes back and leaves the boy behind; if he gets off free, and, dead or alive, fails to restore the boy to me; murder him yourself. And do it the moment he sets foot in this room, or mind me, it will be too late!'

'What is this?'

'What is it?' pursued Fagin, raging. 'I'll tell you what it is. That boy is worth hundreds of pounds to me; am I to lose what chance alone has thrown to me; am I to lose it through the whims of a drunken gang that I could whistle away the lives of! I am bound to that born devil that only wants the....' Panting for breath, the old man stammered for a word; and in that instant checked the torrent of his wrath, and changed his demeanour. In the moments before, his clenched hands had grasped at the air; his eyes had dilated; and his face grown livid; but now, he shrunk into a chair, and, cowering, trembled with the realisation that he had disclosed some hidden villainy of his own. After a short silence, he looked at the young woman, and was reassured on seeing her in the same listless attitude from which he had first roused her.

'Nancy, dear!' he croaked in his usual voice. 'Did you mind me?'

'Don't worry Fagin!' replied the girl, raising her head languidly. 'If Bill has not done it this time, he will another. He has done many a good job for you, and will do many more when he can.'

'Regarding the boy...,' said Fagin, rubbing the palms of his hands nervously together.

'The boy must take his chances with the rest,' interrupted Nancy; 'and I say again, I hope he is dead, because then he will be out of harm's way, and out of yours, - that is, if Bill comes to no harm. And if Toby got clear off, Bill's pretty sure to be safe; for Bill's worth two of Toby any time.'

'And about what I was saying, my dear?' observed Fagin, keeping his glistening eye steadily upon her.

'You must say it all over again, if it's anything you want me to do,' replied Nancy; 'I cannot rouse myself, and I think I'm going deaf in one ear, so I scarcely heard you.'

Fagin put several other questions to which she was so utterly unmoved, that his original impression of her being more than a trifle in liquor, was confirmed. In this Nancy was not exempt from a failing which was very common among all of Fagin's female pupils; and in which, in their tenderer years, they were rather encouraged - to keep them soft and pliant.

Her disordered appearance, and a Geneva perfume which pervaded the whole apartment, seemed to give strong confirmation of Fagin's supposition; she had subsided first into dullness and, afterwards, into a compound of feelings: under the influence of which she shed tears one minute, and in the next gave utterance to various exclamations of 'Never say die!'

Fagin, who had had considerable experience of such matters in his time, saw, with satisfaction, that she was very far gone indeed. This eased his mind; and having accomplished his object of imparting to the girl what he had heard, and of ascertaining, with his own eyes, that Sikes had not returned, Fagin, leaving his young friend asleep with her head upon the table, left to return home.

It was within an hour of midnight. The night was dark and the weather piercing cold, the sharp wind that scoured the streets, seemed to have cleared them, for few people were abroad, and of those that were, all seemed to be hastening home. He had reached the corner of his street, and was fumbling in his pocket for the door-key, when a dark figure emerged from an entrance which lay in deep shadow, and, crossing the road, glided up to him silently.

'Fagin!' whispered a voice close to his ear.

'Ah!' said Fagin, turning quickly round, 'is that you? Bill...?'

What followed need not concern us further here. But shortly after Bill Sikes was taken ill and, being laid up for a week, he was constantly attended to by Nancy, they had to change the location of their rooms; it was even meaner than their last place since it had only a single table, two chairs and a bed; their condition had taken a turn for the worse since the failure of Bill Sikes last 'crack'.

The housebreaker was lying on the bed, wrapped in his everyday great-coat, by way of a dressing-gown, his features were in no degree improved by the cadaverous hue brought on by the illness. He now wore a stiff, black beard of a week's growth.

Nancy sat by the single small window set in the roof, and busily patched an old checked waistcoat which was a part of the robber's attire. She was pale and reduced with watching over him, and from her own privation, since she had been deprived of an income while she had watched and nursed him. She was so pale and reduced that there would have been considerable difficulty in recognising her as the same Nancy who had acted with such a spirited display before, but for the voice in which she replied to Sikes's question.

'It's not long gone seven,' said the girl. 'How do you feel, Bill?'

'As weak as water,' replied Mr Sikes, 'Here; lend us a hand, and let me get off this bed anyhow.'

The illness had not improved Sikes's temper; for, as the girl raised him up and led him to a chair, he muttered various curses on her awkwardness, and struck her, as though by clumsy accident, with his elbow to her head.

'Whining are you?' said Sikes. 'Don't stand snivelling. If you can't do anything better than that, leave it off altogether. D'ye hear me?'

'I hear,' replied the girl, turning her face aside, and forcing a laugh. She stopped laughing and stood silently by him.

'Thought better of it, have you?' growled Sikes. 'All the better for you.' He marked the tear which glistened n her eye, and marked how it trembled there, ready to spillover and streak her cheek. 'An' I'll 'ave no tears, neither,' he added in the same growl.

'Why, you don't mean to say, you'd be hard on me to-night, Bill,' said the girl, laying her hand on his shoulder. 'Look how I've tended to you this past week, and how I'm tending to you now.'

'Why not?' cried Sikes.

'Such a number of nights I've been nursing and caring for you, as if you had been a child of mine,' said the girl, with a touch of woman's tenderness, which added something like a sweetness of tone even to her voice: 'and this is the first that I've seen you like your old self; you wouldn't have treated me as you just did, if you'd thought of that, would you? Come; say you wouldn't.'

'Well, then,' Sikes said, 'I wouldn't? I wouldn't.'

Nancy gave out with a reflexive, though suppressed, sob; but it was not a sob of distress, it was in recognition of what she took to be her paramour's acknowledgment, in those few gruff words, of her aid.

'Why, damme, the girls's whining again!'

'It's nothing,' said the girl, throwing herself into a chair. 'Don't you mind me. It'll soon be over.' She paused, as she wiped her cheek of the offending tear that streaked it. 'It'll soon be over,' she repeated in a reflective whisper.

'What'll be over?' demanded Sikes in a savage voice. 'What foolery are you up to? Don't come over me with any more of your woman's nonsense.'

She waved her hand feebly. 'The illness, Bill. The illness, that's all I meant by it.'

At any other time the tone in which Sikes comment was delivered would have had the desired effect; but the girl being weak and exhausted, dropped her head on the back of the chair, and fainted; it was so sudden that Sikes could not get out even a few of his usual oaths. Not knowing what to do, he resorted to the special care that various expressions of blasphemy might bring: and finding that this treatment was also ineffectual, he called for assistance.

'What's the matter here, my dear?' said Fagin, looking in.

'Lend a hand, can't you?' replied Sikes impatiently.

With an exclamation of surprise, Fagin came to the girl's assistance, while Mr. John Dawkins (otherwise the Artful Dodger), who had followed his friend into the room, hastily snatched a bottle from the grasp of Master Charles Bates who came in also, uncorked it, and poured a portion of its contents down the patient's throat: previously taking a taste himself, to prevent mistakes.

'Don't be out of temper, my dear,' urged Fagin, submissively. 'I have never forgot you, Bill; never once.'

'You've been scheming and plotting every hour that I have laid shivering and burning; and Bill was to do this; and Bill was to do that; and Bill was to do it all dirt cheap, as soon as he got well,' replied Sikes, with a bitter grin. 'Well I've had enough of your work. If it hadn't been for Nance, I might have died.'

'There now, Bill,' remonstrated Fagin, eagerly catching at the word. 'If it hadn't been for Nance! Who but poor old Fagin was the means of your having such a handy girl about you?'

'True enough!' said Nancy, coming forward. Nancy's appearance gave a new turn to the conversation; for the boys, receiving a sly wink from the Fagin, began to ply her with liquor: however, although she took it, it was only sparingly; while Fagin, continuously pouring out an unusual flow of spirits upon Sikes, gradually brought him into a better temper, by seeming to regard his threats as just a little pleasant banter.

'It's all very well,' said Sikes; 'but I must have some blunt from you to-night.'

'I haven't a piece of coin about me,' replied Fagin.

'You've got lots at home,' retorted Sikes; 'and I must have some from there.'

'Lots!' cried Fagin, holding up is hands. 'I haven't so much as....'

'I don't know how much you've got, and I dare say you hardly know yourself, as it would take a pretty long time to count it,' said Sikes; 'but I must have some to-night; and that's flat.'

'Well, well,' said Fagin, with a sigh, 'I'll send the Artful round.'

'You won't do nothing of the kind,' replied Sikes. 'The Artful's a deal too artful, and would lose his way, or get dodged by traps, or anything for an excuse, if you put him to it. Nancy shall go and fetch it, to make sure; and I'll have a snooze while she's gone.'

After a deal of haggling and squabbling, Fagin beat down the amount of the required advance from five pounds to three pounds four and sixpence: protesting that that would only leave him eighteen-pence to keep house with; Mr Sikes sullenly remarked that if he couldn't get any more he must get his club and accompany Fagin home. Fagin assured him that he would comply and have the money advanced to him that night. Mr Sikes flung himself on the bed to sleep away the time until the young lady's return. In obedience to this hint, the boys, nodding to Nancy, took up their hats, and left the room and together with Fagin returned home.

'Now,' said Fagin, when they had arrived 'I'll get that cash. This is only the key of a little cupboard where I keep a few odd things the boys get, my dear. I never lock up my money, because I've got none to lock up - ha! ha! ha! It's a poor trade, Nancy, and there are no thanks; but I'm fond of seeing the young people about me; and I bear it, I bear it all. Hush!' he said, hastily concealing the key in his breast; 'Listen! who's that?'

The girl, who had come in and sat at the table with her arms folded, appeared not to be interested in the arrival: or to care whether the person, whoever he was, came or went: until the murmur of a man's voice reached her ears. The instant she caught the sound, she tore off her bonnet and shawl, and thrust them under the table.

"It's the man I expected; he's come,' he whispered, as though nettled by the interruption, 'Not a word about the money while he's here, Nance. He won't stop long, my dear.' Laying his boney forefinger upon his lip, Fagin carried a candle to the door. He reached it at the same moment as the visitor, who, coming into the room, was close to the girl before he observed her.

It was Monks.

On seeing Nancy sitting in the room the visitor drew back, Fagin said to him, 'Don't worry. One of my young people,'

The girl glanced at Monks with an air of carelessness, and looked away; but as he turned towards Fagin, she took another look; keen and searching, and full of purpose. The girl then drew closer to the table, and made no offer to leave the room, although she could see that Monks in his gestures and expression wished her to. Fagin pointed upward to an upper room, and took Monks out.

'Not that hole we were in before,' she could hear the man say as they went upstairs. Fagin laughed; and made some reply which did not reach her.

Before the sound of their footsteps had ceased to sound through the house, the girl had slipped off her shoes; she glided from the room and ascended the stairs with great softness and silence, one of the skills that she had been tutored in by Mr Nathanial Fagin himself. She stood at the door, listening with breathless interest.

'Why not have made a sneaking, snivelling pickpocket of him?' she heard the visitor say.

'Hear him!' exclaimed Nat Fagin.

'Do you mean to say you couldn't have done it?' demanded the other. 'Haven't you done it, with other boys, scores of times?

'Whose turn would that have served, my dear?' inquired the Jew.

'Mine,' replied Monks.

'But not mine,' said Fagin. 'When there are two parties to a bargain, it is only reasonable that the interests of both should be consulted; isn't it? I saw it was not easy to train him to the business, he was not like the other boys. I had no hold over him to make him worse,' pursued Fagin. 'His hand was not in. I had nothing to frighten him with; which we always must have in the beginning, or we labour in vain. What could I do? Send him out with the Dodger and Charley? We had enough of that before; I trembled for us all then.'

'That was not my doing,' observed the other.

'No, no, my dear!' renewed Fagin. 'If it had never happened, you might never have clapped eyes on the boy, and so led to the discovery that it was him you were looking for. Well! I got him back for you by means of Nancy; and then she begins to favour him.'

'Throttle the girl!' said Monks, impatiently.

'Why, we can't afford to do that, besides, that sort of thing is not in our way; otherwise I might be glad to have it done. I know what these girls are like, Monks. As soon as the boy begins to harden, she'll care no more for him than you would for a block of wood. You want him made a thief. If he is still alive, I can make him one and... if the worst comes to the worst, and he is dead....'

'It's no fault of mine if he is!' interposed the other man 'Mind that. Fagin! I had no hand in it. Anything but his death, I told you from the first. I won't shed blood; it's always found out, and besides, it haunts a man. If they shot him dead, I was not the cause; hear me?

So they went on, so that the downstairs room remained deserted for a quarter of an hour or more; the girl glided back with the same unearthly tread; and, immediately afterwards, the two men descended. Monks went on into the street; and Fagin returned upstairs again for the money. When he returned to the room downstairs, the girl was adjusting her shawl and bonnet, as if preparing to be gone.

'Why, Nance!' exclaimed Fagin, starting back, 'how pale you are!'

'Pale?' echoed the girl, shading her eyes with her hands, as if to look steadily at him.

'Quite horrible. What have you been doing?'

'Nothing that I know of, except sitting in this place for I don't know how long,' replied the girl carelessly. 'Come! Let me get back to my place; there's a dear.'

With a sigh for every piece of money, Fagin told the amount into her hand. They parted without further conversation, and she did not return his 'good-night.'

When the girl got into the street, she sat upon a doorstep; and seemed bewildered. Suddenly she rose; and hurried on: she soon reached their dwelling place.

If she betrayed agitation to Sikes, he did not observe it; he merely inquired if she had brought the money, it being the greater of his concerns, and on receiving the reply that she had, he uttered his satisfaction in the form of a growl, and replaced his head upon the pillow, and resumed his slumbers.

It became known to Fagin's gang that Oliver was in the care of the family of Miss Rose Maylie. Nancy knew that Nat Fagin intended to get the boy into his gang again, and that the mysterious Monks had a hand in the design.

She, who had never 'snitched' on the gang before, and did not intend to do so now, nonetheless wished to inform Miss Rose Maylie of what was afoot, so that the boy may be saved from being forced back into the company and form of living that had been her lot.

Why this was can only be speculated at; it may have been as simple as, no matter how roughly life had dealt with her, there was something about the boy, an affecting simplicity or innocence that appealed to a young woman's sentimental heart, even in that place where it may be supposed that there was no room or rightful place for sentimentality, certainly not as any gentle-folk could comprehend. Nonetheless, there it was. This motivated her actions.

It was fortunate for her that the possession of money kept Bill, on the next day, in the important employment of eating and drinking; it had a great beneficial effect in smoothing down, that is, improving his temper.

Nancy had about her all the abstracted and nervous manner of one who is on the eve of some bold and hazardous step - it would have been obvious to the lynx-eyed Fagin, who would most probably have taken the alarm at once; but that was not so for Mr Sikes, who lacked such niceties of character that would enable him to identify the like. Furthermore, the food and drink ensured that he was in an unusually amiable condition, so that he saw nothing unusual in her demeanour, and troubled himself so little about her, that, had her agitation been more perceptible than it was, it would still not have been likely to have awakened his suspicions.

The girl's excitement increased as night came on. She sat watching until the housebreaker drank himself asleep. But there came such an unusual paleness to her cheek, and a fire in her eye, that even Sikes observed it with astonishment. Sikes, being still weak from the fever, was lying in bed, taking hot water with his gin to render it less inflammatory; and had pushed his glass towards Nancy to be replenished.

'Why, burn my body!' said the man, raising himself as he stared the girl in the face. 'You look like a corpse come to life. What's the matter?'

'Matter!' replied the girl. 'Nothing. What do you look at me so hard for?'

'What foolery is this?' demanded Sikes, grasping her by the arm, and shaking her roughly. 'What is it? What are you thinking of?'

'Of many things, Bill,' replied the girl, shivering, and as she did so, pressed her hands upon her eyes, and the side of her head. 'But, what is odd in that?'

The tone of forced gaiety in which she spoke these words, seemed to produce a deeper impression on Sikes than her wild look.

'I tell you wot it is,' said Sikes; 'if you haven't caught fever, and got it comin' on, now. There's something dangerous in it,' said Sikes, fixing his eyes upon her, and muttering the words to himself; 'There ain't a stauncher-hearted gal going, or I'd have cut her throat months ago. She's got the fever; that's all it is.'

Fortifying himself with this assurance, Sikes drained the glass, and called again for his physic. The girl quickly poured out another glass with her back towards him; he held the vessel to his lips and drank off the contents.

'Now,' said the robber, 'come on the bed and sit by me, and put on your own face; or I'll alter it so, that you won't know it agin.'

The girl obeyed. Sikes, put his left arm around her waist, and took a firm hold of her arm by the wrist, with his right hand, and twisted it behind her back; but before he could hold her in this posture for more than a few moments he fell back upon the cushion: turning his eyes upon her face. They closed; opened again; closed once more; again opened. He shifted his position restlessly; and, after dozing a few more moments, and springing up with a look of terror while gazing vacantly about him, he raised his arm to strike her.

'Wot 'ave you done?' he gasped before he slumped back, being so suddenly stricken into a deep and heavy sleep. The upraised arm fell by his side. The grasp of his hand relaxed enough for her to extricate her wrist from his grip; and he lay like one in a profound trance.

'The laudanum,' murmured the girl, as she rose from the bedside. 'But I may be too late, even now.'

She dressed in her bonnet and shawl: looking around with fear from time to time, as if, despite the sleeping draught, she expected to feel Sikes's heavy hand come down upon her; then, stooping over the bed she kissed his lips, as was her habit whether she was bruised or not. She opened the door with a noiseless touch and hurried from the house.

As she passed down a dark passageway a watchman was crying half-past nine.

'Has it long gone the half-hour?' asked the girl.

'It'll strike the hour in another quarter,' said the man: raising his lantern to her face.

'And I cannot get there in less than an hour,' muttered Nancy: brushing swiftly past him and gliding down the street. Many of the shops were already closing in the back lanes and avenues from Spitalfields towards the West End of London. As she rushed along the pavement the clock struck ten, increasing her impatience. she tore along the narrow streets: elbowing others; and darting almost under the horses' heads, as she crossed the crowded roads, where clusters of people were eagerly watching their opportunity to do the like.

When she reached the wealthier quarter of town, the streets were comparatively deserted. Her destination was a family hotel in a quiet but handsome street near Hyde Park. As the brilliant light of the lamp which burnt above its door, guided her, the clock struck eleven. Having hurried so far, she loitered for a few paces as though irresolute; she spat the thick phlegm, that had come to her mouth from having to rush, into the gutter and, on making up her mind, she stepped into the hall. She glanced at the porter's seat as she passed and was relieved to see it was vacant. She advanced towards the stairs.

'Now, now young woman!' said a smartly-dressed female, looking out from a door behind her, 'what is it that you want here?'

'A lady who is stopping in here,' she answered.

'A lady? What lady?'

'Miss Maylie,' said Nancy.

The woman, who had by this time noted her appearance, replied only by a look of virtuous disdain; and summoned a man. To him, Nancy repeated her request.

'What name am I to say?' asked the waiter.

'It's of no use saying any, she doesn't know me,' replied Nancy.

'Nor business?' said the man.

'No, nor that,' replied the girl. 'But I must see the lady.'

'Come!' said the man, pushing her towards the door. 'None of this. Take yourself off.'

'I shall be carried out if I go!' said the girl, her voice rising in pitch; 'and I can make that a job that two of you won't like to do. Isn't there anybody here,' she said, looking round, 'that will see a simple message carried for a poor wretch like me?'

This appeal produced an effect on a good-tempered-faced man-cook, who was looking on, and who stepped forward.

'Take it up for her, Joe; can't you?' he said.

'What's the good?' replied the man. 'Look at her. You don't suppose any young lady will see such as her; do you?'

To this Nancy's doubtful character, raised a quantity of chaste wrath in the bosoms of four housemaids, who remarked that the creature was a disgrace to their sex; and advocated her being thrown into the kennel.

'Do what you like with me,' said the girl, otherwise ignoring them, and turning to the men again; 'but do as I ask of you, and I ask you to give this message for God Almighty's sake.'

The soft-hearted cook interceded again, the result was that the man who had first appeared undertook its delivery.

'What's it to be?' said the man, with one foot on the stairs.

'That a young woman earnestly asks to speak to Miss Rose Maylie alone,' said Nancy; 'and if the lady will only hear the first word she has to say, she will know whether to hear her business in full, or to have her turned out of doors.'

'I say,' said the man, 'you're coming it strong!'

'Give the message,' said the girl firmly; 'and let me hear the answer.'

The man ran upstairs. Nancy remained, almost breathless and pale, listening to the very audible and prolific expressions of scorn, of the chaste housemaids. She, unaccustomedly, quailed at their comments - being, as she was, far away from her world - but she assumed the hard face of contempt that was usual when confronted with these expressions of disdain.

When the man returned, he said she was to walk upstairs.

-'It's no good being proper in this world,' said the first housemaid.

-'Brass can do better than gold what has stood the fire,' said the second.

-'I can't help wondering what ladies was made of', the third contented herself with.

Nancy followed the man, with trembling limbs, to a small ante-chamber. Here he left her. The room was lighted by a single gas lamp from the ceiling. She had never been in a room with such bright lights as this and stood looking at the gas lamp as she waited.

This girl's life had been squandered on the streets, and among the most noisome of the stews and dens of London too, but there was something of her original nature still left; and when she heard a light step approaching the door, and thought of the wide contrast of their circumstances, materially and morally, she felt burdened with the sense of her own deep shame, and nearly turned to run, despite all her resolve; as though she could scarcely bear the presence of her with whom she had sought this interview. But struggling against these feelings there was Pride, the vice of the lowest and most debased no less than of the high and self-assured. While it was true that she was the miseried companion of thieves and ruffians, the outcast of even the lowest haunts, the associate of the scourings of jails and hulks, always living within the shadow of the gallows, yet, even this young woman felt too proud to betray a feeble gleam of the womanly feeling (which she thought a weakness, but which alone connected her with humanity, and was proof of that connection), of which her wasting life had obliterated so many, many traces when still a child.

So, instead, she raised her head and levelled her eyes to observe the figure which presented itself; it was that of a slight and beautiful girl who was in the lovely bloom and spring-time of young womanhood; the young lady's deep blue eyes shone with intelligence and sympathy, and a shadow of wariness, so Nancy perceived it; it was as though one of God's angels had been enthroned in mortal form and placed upon the earth, for His good purposes, if one may suggest this, without the charge of impiety to be brought. This is how it seemed to Nancy at that moment, this being only an indication of the degree that she was taken aback at this sight. The young woman was probably not past seventeen, she estimated; not far from her own age, but so very different in every apparent form, dress, condition and circumstance. Rose Maylie was cast in so slight and exquisite a mould; and presented so mild and gentle, so pure and beautiful an impression, that earth seemed to not be her true element, nor its rough creatures her fit companions; a sensation that deepened the wretched visitors sense of the natural gulf between them.

So many of these marks of fine grace, especially the smallness and the fragility of her frame, were the residue of a grave illness that had beset her not more than four months beforehand; her physical shape had been much reduced and she was far from fully restored, and her manner was much altered by her knowledge of how closely she had come to a flower ornamented summer grave. With this knowledge, she had resolved that, if she should live, she would seek to aid those that needed it, as far as it was possible for her to do so.

Yet Nancy could not know this, and had a shrinking sense in her presence; she fell back on Pride. She cast her eyes to the ground for a moment, tossed her head with affected carelessness and said: 'It's a hard matter to get to see you, lady. If I had taken offence, and gone away, as many would have done, you'd have been sorry for it, and not without reason.'

'I am sorry if anyone has behaved harshly to you,' replied Rose. 'I am the person you inquired for. Tell me, please, why you wish to see me.'

The tone of this answer, the sweet voice uncaged from the lovely mouth with the lovely arcing bow of her lips, the gentle manner, the absence of haughtiness at being presented into her own appalling company, her docile eyes; all this took the girl wholly by surprise; it accentuated the contrast in their positions in the entire histories of their lives to this point of their meeting still further; all this overcame her own Pride and her practised stubborn defiance, and she burst into tears.

'Oh, lady!' she said, clasping her hands over her face, 'if there was more like you, there would be fewer like me - oh, there would! - there would!'

'Sit down. Please,' said Rose. 'If you are in poverty or affliction I shall endeavour to relieve you if I can.'

'Let me stand,' said the girl, still weeping, 'But it is not poverty that has brought me to seek you, though I know the gnawing truth of it, right enough; it may the appearance of things, but it is not that which brings me here. And, please, do not speak to me so kindly...'

'I must speak to you as I must, in the manner which is in keeping with my nature...'

'But, still, please do not.'

'Will you not sit down.'

Nancy was ready to refuse, but the anxiety that preceded her rush to this location, her dash to get here, and the dizzy light-headedness she experienced lately from Bill's beatings, mounted and nearly overcame her.

'I will sit,' she said as though she were making a very great concession; and she sat on a deeply upholstered chair, though only perching herself on the edge of it.

'If it is not poverty, then why have you asked to see me?'

'Is - is - that door shut?'

The young lady affirmed that it was.

'I am about to put my life, and the lives of others, in your hands, by coming here to tell you what I am about to,' the girl said. 'I am the girl that dragged little Oliver away on the night he went out from the house in Pentonville.

'You!' said Rose.

'Aye, it was!' replied the girl. 'And I can't tell you how much I regret it now, for it was I that brought him back into the company of thieves and housebreakers, and the consequence is that he was shot, nearly to death, on that job in Chertsey. It was not by design, but I played my part. I am the infamous creature you have heard of from witnesses. How I wish I had no hand in it, for there are things I must tell you that causes such as I to tremble for fear and anger. Yes, one such as I, who lives among thieves, and that never from the first moment I can recollect have known a better life, or kinder words, than you have just spoken to me, so help me! Do not mind shrinking from me, lady. I am the sort that is known - or condemned - as 'debased' and 'ruined', but I am what I am; I could say that it's not such a bad life, having known no other; and by that admission I know I am not for good ladies like you to mix with. But, for the part I had in abducting Oliver, I'll have no further truck. And for what I have just confessed to being a part of, it is a wonder to me that you do not shrink! I am younger than you would think to look at me. Even the poorest women recoil from me and the likes of me, as I make my way along the crowded pavement. Thank Heaven, dear lady,' continued the girl, 'that you had friends to care for you and keep you, and that you were never in the midst of cold and hunger, and riot and drunkenness, and - and - worse than all that - as I have been from the time I was lifted out of my cradle. If I ever had such as a cradle, it was the alley and the gutter that were my cradle, as they will be my deathbed.'

'I have pity for you!' said Rose, her voice breaking with a sudden sincere surge of that emotion.

'Heaven bless you!' Nancy replied, and she realised that, if it had not been for the beguiling appearance of the young lady, and the purpose of her visit, that she would have, in every other circumstance, flung such words back in anyone else's face who had used them to her; and with an additional garnishing of oaths too. 'If you knew what I was, you would turn away. Still, I have come from those who would surely murder me if they knew I were here, to tell you what I must. Do you know a man named Monks?'

'No,' said Rose.

'No matter,' replied the girl. 'He knows you, and knew you were here, for it was by hearing him tell of this place that I found you.'

'I have never heard the name,' said Rose.

'Then he must go by some other name amongst us,' replied the girl, 'Some time ago, and soon after Oliver was put into your house after the robbery, I - suspecting this man - listened to a conversation between him and another. I found out that Monks had seen him, accidently, with two of our boys on the day we lost him, and had known him to be the child that he was watching out for, though I couldn't make out why. A bargain was struck with a man named Fagin, that if Oliver was got back he should have a certain sum. And he was to have more for making him a thief, which is what this Monks wanted, for some purpose of his own.'

'For what purpose?' asked Rose.

'I could not guess let alone know, until last night when he came again. I listened at the door. The first words I heard Monks say were these: "So the only proofs of the boy lie at the bottom of the river, and the old hag that received them from the mother is rotting in her coffin." They laughed, and talked of his success in doing this; and Monks, talking on about the boy, and getting very wild, said that though he had got the young devil's money now, he'd rather have had it another way; for, what a game it would have been to have brought down the boast of his father's will, by driving him through every jail in town, and then hauling him up for some capital felony, which Fagin could easily manage, after having made a good profit off him. Then he said, that if he could gratify his hatred by taking the boy's life without bringing his own neck in danger, he would; but, as he couldn't, he'd look to meet him at every turn in his life; and would take advantage of his birth and history, and he might harm him yet. "In short, Fagin," he says, "you never laid such snares as I'll contrive for my own young brother, Oliver."'

'His brother!' exclaimed Rose.

'Those were his own words, miss,' said Nancy, glancing uneasily round, for a vision of Sikes perpetually haunted her. 'And more. When he spoke of you, and said it seemed contrived by Heaven, or the devil, against him, that Oliver should come into the hands of those that would act as his protectors, he laughed, and said there was some comfort in that too, for how many thousands and hundreds of thousands of pounds would you not give, if you had them, to know who your two-legged spaniel really was.'

'This was said in earnest?' said Rose, turning pale.

'He spoke in hard earnest, if a man ever did,' replied the girl. 'He is an earnest man, and his hatred is up. I know his kind all to well, and I know many who do worse things; but I'd rather listen to them a dozen times, than to that Monks once more. It is growing late, and I have to reach home without suspicion of having been on such an errand as this. I must get back quickly.'

'What use can I turn your information to without you?' said Rose. 'And you would wish to go back? Why do you wish to return to such companions that you paint in such terrible colours? If you repeat this to a gentleman whom I can summon in an instant from the next room, you can be consigned to some place of safety without half an hour's delay.'

'I wish to go back,' said the girl. 'I must go back, because - how can I tell such things to an innocent like you - because among the men I have told you of, there is one: the most desperate among them; that I can't leave.' She paused, and a quizzical expression crossed her face. 'No, I can't leave him,' she repeated, as if to reaffirm this grim knowledge to herself, as a final recognition and acknowledgement, 'not even to be saved from the life I am leading.' She felt, and then rubbed, the right side of her face.

'Your coming here, at so great a risk to tell me what you have heard; your manner; convinces me of the truth; your evident contrition and sense of shame; all lead me to believe that you might yet be reclaimed,' said the earnest young lady, as the tears coursed down her face, 'do not turn a deaf ear to the entreaties of one of your own sex; one who now appeals to you in the voice of pity and compassion. Hear me, let me save you yet, for better things.'

'Lady,' sobbed the girl, 'dear, sweet, angel lady. We are of the same sex, true, yet I am so different from you, brought up by all the struggles and contrivances of survival alone. You are the first that ever blessed me with such words, and if I had heard them ten years ago, they might have turned me from my life as I now lead it; but it is too late, it is too late!'

'It is never too late,' said Rose, 'You have come here to volunteer this intelligence, it cannot be too late for the good in you to bloom further. To do so indicates to me that there is surely room for penitence and atonement also.'

'It is too late, though I wish I could say otherwise; I cannot. I cannot leave him! Them things,' the young wretch said, 'penitence and atonement, they're not for me, I am far beyond them. Even less so if I were the cause of his death, and I could not be his death.'

'Why should you be?' asked Rose.

'Given his life, there is nothing that would be said in a courtroom that could save him,' the girl said, coming close to sobbing again. 'If I told any others what I have told you, and it led to their being taken, he would be sure to hang. Many a young man, all friends of mine, have died because of how they have lived. He has been so cruel, but he is the boldest of them all! The best to be with, and I have the bruises and cuts as proof of that.'

'I cannot understand it. Is it possible that, for such a man, you can resign every future hope, and the certainty of immediate rescue? I offer that now. Do not go back to him that reduces you to misery. It is a form of madness to resist rescue.'

'I don't know what it is,' answered the girl; 'I only know that it is so, and that is not only so for me alone, but with hundreds of others like me, all as wretched as myself. Perhaps it is by this truth, as much as by our lives and livelihoods, that makes us so wretched; but I *must* go back to him. Whether it is God's wrath for the wrongs I have done, I do not know; but I am drawn back to him, regardless of every suffering and ill use he causes me. Even though I know that, at the last, I may die by his hand.'

'This is too appalling. What am I to do?' said Rose; in a moment she seemed to be resolved, she walked to the door that the other young woman had entered by, and there she stood as if to bar her exit. 'If nothing else, I shall not let you depart from me.'

'You must, and you will,' the girl continued. 'I would not be stopped in getting in to see you and deliver this errand, nor will you stop my going my own way; I have trusted in your goodness, and forced no promise from you, as I might have done.'

'Of what use, then, is the communication you have made?' asked Rose. 'This mystery must be investigated, or how will your disclosure to me, benefit Oliver, whom you are clearly willing to serve?'

'You must have a confidante about you that will hear it as a secret, and advise you what to do,' said the girl.

'But where can I find you again when necessary?' asked Rose. 'I do not seek to know where you live, but where will you be that a further meeting be set?'

'Will you promise me that you will have my secret strictly kept, and come alone, or with the only other person that knows it; and that I shall not be watched or followed?' asked the girl.

'I promise you this most solemnly,' answered Rose.

'Then,' said the girl without hesitation, 'each Sunday night, from eleven until the clock strikes twelve, I will walk on London Bridge; if I am alive.'

'If you are alive!' repeated Rose, realising suddenly, with fuller horror, the possibility of immediate danger this wretched young woman had subjected herself to. 'Stay!' Rose implored, as the girl moved hurriedly to exit. 'Think again on your own condition, and the opportunity you have of escaping it. You have a claim on me: not only as the voluntary bearer of this intelligence, but as a woman who may think she is lost beyond redemption; but redemption is boundless, and you must surely remain within the bounds of it by this voluntary act alone. Must you return to this gang of robbers, and to this one man, who seems to have a fiendish hold over you, or a spell upon you? A word can save you! What fascination is it that can take you back, and make you cling to wickedness and misery? Is there no chord in your heart that I can pluck! Is there nothing to which I can appeal against your dreadful infatuation!'

'When ladies as young, and good, and beautiful as you,' replied the girl steadily, 'give away your hearts, love will carry you - yes, even such as you , who have home, hearth, family, friends, and many other admirers, everything, to fill them. When such as I, whose only certainties are a temporary room and the lid of a coffin, and no certain friend in sickness or death but the charity nurse, set our ruined and rotten hearts on a man, any man, ruined and rotten as he will be, and let him fill the place that has been a blank from our wretched childhoods, who can hope to cure us? Pity us, lady. Pity those of us for having this one feeling that a woman can ever own, and that is all that is left to us; and pity us the more for having even that one blessing in our lives turned, by their heavy hands, from a comfort and a pride, into another means of desperate suffering.'

'You will,' said Rose, after a pause, 'take some money from me, which may enable you to live without dishonesty - at all events until we meet again?'

'Not a penny,' replied the girl adamantly, waving her hand.

'Do not close your heart against all my efforts to help you.'

'I do not; but I came here to help you, I did not come to seek your help. I can earn my keep and have no need of charity,' she said, her former Pride flaring for an instant, as a coal upon a fire may flare and spit.

Rose, stepped gently forward and said 'Do not say charity; since as you say yourself, you can earn your keep; you said that if I knew what you were that I would turn away from you. But, if I may venture it, what you do to earn a living is you offer as a service, yes? I know what you are, and I do not turn away...'

'Please, say no more of it,' pleaded the girl in the sudden renewal of the agony of recognition of the gulf between them, and also in being struck by the unfamiliarity of the kindness with which the young lady spoke to her.

'Take a payment,' Rose Maylie insisted, 'not as a gift nor as charity, but for the service you have done by coming here with this information.'

The girl comprehended the sense and reason in what was said and hesitated a moment, but rejected it. 'No; I live as I have always lived, by any and every means, and always with a price on everything; this I offer without a price.'

'I cannot share sufferings such as yours...' said the young lady.

'And I bless God, and you should always thank God, that you do not,' Nancy burst out.

'...but how can I best alleviate some part of your burden. For what you have told me, I wish to serve you indeed.'

'You would serve me best,' replied the girl, 'if you could take my life at once; for I have felt more grief to think of what I am, in meeting you tonight, than I ever did before. To pass such as you in the common truck and trade of the streets of the city only deepens the senseless envy in me; to escape that envy it is best to cultivate indifference and then contempt. But I am further blighted, and my resolve is weakened rather than fortified, by being in such close proximity to you, and by the contrast between us; even moreso by the unexpected kindness you have been prepared to show me. It truly would be something not to die in the hell in which I live. But it is a hell I am long since grown used to, and there is no righting that now. God bless you, sweet lady!'

The girl swiftly swerved around the person of Rose Maylie as she stood before the door, and left the room; while the young lady, overpowered by this extraordinary and unexpected meeting, which had more of the semblance of a dream than an occurrence, sank into a chair, and endeavoured to collect her wandering thoughts. Her situation was one of no common trial and difficulty. While she felt the eager desire to penetrate the mystery in which Oliver's history was enveloped, she could not but hold sacred the confidence which this miserable woman had rested in her, moreso since she recognised how much of a young and guileless girl she herself was when compared to the life that her wretched informant had led, and still led, though she was not much older than herself. Her words and manner had touched Rose so that her wish to win the outcast back to hope and repentance was scarcely less intense. Then she felt that she would rather win her back to hope, more than repentance; she realised that the girl had sincerely meant that repentance was beyond her, but what wounded Rose to the greater degree was comprehending that the girl was utterly without hope. To restore her to hope would be the finer endeavour to succeed in.

Rose had intended to remain in London only three days. It was now midnight of the first day. What course of action could she determine upon, which could be adopted in forty-eight hours. Disturbed by her reflections; inclining now to one course and then to another, and recoiling from each, as the difficulties associated with each consideration presented itself to her mind; Rose passed a sleepless and anxious night.

Nancy kept a print in the room she shared with Bill Sikes, but it was not one that was kept in a frame and hung upon the wall; they kept no such items upon their walls; she kept it between two sheets of thick card, so it shouldn't be damaged, and always put it under the mattress so that it lay flat against the bed frame; she would take it out from this place, when Bill wasn't at home, and she would look at it.

She had recovered it from a copy of The Journal of Herriot's Literary & Arts Society which she had found discarded in the street on an occasion, not much more than a year previously, when she had walked up to the fashionable part of the city. On one side of the sheet of paper were two images, one was of a storm over a mountain in the Scottish Highlands, the other was of a busy scene at a horse racing course. But it was the image on the other side of the sheet that she kept it for. Although she could only read in the most rudimentary fashion, she had consequently struggled with the accompanying caption until she understood that the print was of an engraving taken from a painting by William Forth; it was of a young woman, indeed it was the artist's fiance. In this image she saw a form of life so removed from that known to herself that it might as well have been the life of someone who lived upon the moon. Rather than regard the subject, the woman in the image, with her ordinary contempt, or envy, or with her customary deliberate assumed indifference, she could not help herself but admire the young woman depicted in the print.

The woman's hair was long and straight, dark and glossy, and it was worn with a centre parting and drawn back from her face. She sat upon an ornately carved chair and was leaning up against, and rested on, a deep red cushion. Her shoulders were narrow but plump and rounded, her forearms were bare and she held a small pink rose in one hand. She wore a perfectly white dress that matched the tone of her skin; Nancy had scarcely seen anything so white and clean, in either the dress or the girl; nothing could be kept clean in the neighbourhoods she lived in; and she had lived in many, and moved through many more; for while the corner of the city in which she was a habitue was burgeoning with the exchange of goods, and every variety of business and trade, it was generally of the dirtier and squalid sorts. In that print was represented a well-fed and easy contentment, and Nancy saw all that she was not; however, she did not resent it. The face of the young woman always drew her eyes to it; it was the sweetest face she had ever seen, until she had met Rose Maylie.

When she arrived home she was relieved that Bill was still passed out and he remained so for more than an hour; she took the print from the place it was secreted away and gazed at it once again, and kept looking at it until she heard him stirring.

Nancy was not, by nature, inclined to melancholy, or toward feeling sorry for her blighted condition; rather she tended to accept it as a forlorn and unalterable fact, which, indeed, it was. She faced her condition with a scatological form of humour, that the pick-pocket boys especially liked in her and liked her for it. However, between this printed image, and the young lady she had met earlier in the evening, and remembering how that lady had spoken so gently and sympathetically to her, they both accentuated in her consciousness everything she could never be, and for the second time that evening she did something she rarely did; she wept for herself and her bitter plight.

Adept as she was in all the arts of cunning, Nancy could not wholly conceal the effect which the knowledge of the step she had taken wrought upon her mind. Fagin and Sikes had confided to her their schemes, which had, otherwise, been hidden from all others: in the full confidence that she was trustworthy and beyond the reach of suspicion. And now, she knew, she was not beyond that reach - although they had yet to discover it.

Bitter as were her feelings were towards Fagin, who had led her, step-by-step, deeper and deeper into the abyss of misery and crime she inhabited, and from which there was now no escape, and though she wished that he, Fagin, should drop from the gallows platform at last - so richly did he merit the fate - and by her hand; she knew that her own Bill Sikes would also be implicated, so she felt some relenting sense, lest her disclosure should also bring Sikes within the closing clutch of the rope with the slipping knot, that he had so far eluded.

Her fears for Sikes would have been powerful inducements to recoil frm her own action; but she had stipulated that her secret should be kept. Other than her mention of Fagin, she had dropped no further clue which could lead to discovery. She had refused a refuge, even from all the guilt and wretchedness that encompassed her. What more could she do! She was resolved.

Though all her mental struggles terminated in this conclusion, they nonetheless forced themselves upon her, again and again, and left their traces. She grew ever paler and thinner, even within the span of the one week that followed. At times, she took no food at all, and no heed of what was passing before her, or took no part in conversations where once, she would have been the loudest. At other times, she laughed without merriment, and was noisy, while a moment after she sat silent and dejected, brooding with her head upon her hand, while the very effort by which she roused herself told that she was ill, or ill at ease, and that her thoughts were occupied with matters distant from those of her criminal companions.

It was a Sunday night, and the bell of the nearest church struck the hour. Sikes and Fagin were talking. The girl looked up from her low seat and listened. Eleven.

'An hour this side of midnight,' said Sikes, 'Dark and heavy it is too. A good night for business.'

'Ah!' replied Fagin. 'What a pity, Bill, my dear, that there's none as ready as you are for work to be done.'

'It is a pity too,' replied Sikes gruffly, 'for I'm in the humour for it.'

Fagin sighed, and shook his head despondently. He pulled Sikes by the sleeve and pointed his finger towards Nancy, who had taken advantage of their conversation to put on her bonnet, and was leaving the room.

'Hallo!' cried Sikes. 'Nance. Where's the gal going to at this time of night?'

'Not far.'

'What answer's that?' retorted Sikes. 'Where yer goin'?'

'I don't know where,' replied the girl.

'Then I do,' said Sikes, more in the spirit of obstinacy than because he had any real objection to the girl going anywhere. 'Nowhere. Now sit down!'

'I'm not well. I told you that,' replied the girl. 'I want a breath of air.'

'Put your head out of the winder,' replied Sikes.

'There's not enough,' said the girl. 'That's too odious, I need it to be fresh. I want it in the street.'

'Then you won't have it,' replied Sikes. With this assurance he rose and locked the door, took the key out, and pulled her bonnet from her head and flung it down. 'There,' said the robber. 'Now stop quietly where you are, will you?'

'It's not such a matter as a bonnet would keep me in,' said the girl turning very pale. 'What do you mean, Bill? Do you know what you're doing?'

'Know what I'm... Oh!' cried Sikes, turning to Fagin, 'look at 'er, she's out of her senses again, you know, or she daren't talk to me in that way.'

'You'll drive me on to something desperate,' muttered the girl placing both hands upon her breast, as though to force down some violent outbreak. 'Let me go, will you, this minute - this instant.'

'No!' said Sikes.

'Tell him to let me go, Fagin. He had better. It'll be better for him. Do you hear me?' cried Nancy.

'Hear you!' repeated Sikes turning round in his chair to confront her. 'Aye! And if I hear you for half a minute longer, the dog shall have a grip on your throat as'll tear some of that screaming voice out. Wot has come over you, you jade! Wot is it?'

'Let me go,' said the girl; then sitting herself on the floor, at the door, she said, 'Bill, let me go; you don't know what you are doing. You don't, indeed. For only one hour - do - do!'

'Cut my limbs off one-by-one!' cried Sikes, seizing her roughly by the arms, he tried to haul her to her feet but she would not stand upright, she let her legs dangle limply.

'The gal's stark raving mad. Stand on your own two feet, wontcha! Stand up, will you?'

'Not till you let me go - not till you let me go. Never - never!' screamed the girl, still struggling tempestuously in his failing grip. Sikes let go his grip and stood back to look on at her for a minute, watching for his opportunity. Suddenly he leapt at her and pinioned her hands and dragged her, struggling and wrestling with him into a small room adjoining, where he thrust her into a chair and held her down by force.

She struggled and implored by turns until twelve o'clock had struck, and then, wearied and exhausted, ceased to contest the point. He struck her then for causing him so much trouble, and each strike was backed by many oaths and threats of most severe violence; that she should make no more efforts to go out that night. Sikes left her to recover at leisure and rejoined Fagin.

'Whew!' said the housebreaker wiping the perspiration from his face. 'Wot a precious strange gal that is!'

'You may say that, Bill,' replied Fagin thoughtfully. 'You may say that.'

'Wot did she take it into her head to go out to-night for, do you think?' asked Sikes. 'Come; you've known 'er since she was eight - or six years of age , was it? - you should know her better than me. Wot does it mean?'

'Obstinacy; it's woman's obstinacy, I suppose, my dear.'

'Well, I suppose it is,' growled Sikes. 'I thought I had tamed her, and she has the marks to prove the method of my training, and I'd taken it to be a proven success, but she's as bad as ever, lately.'

'Worse,' said Fagin thoughtfully. 'I never knew her like this, and for such a little cause too.'

'Nor I,' said Sikes. 'I think she's got a touch of that fever I 'ad still in her blood yet, and it won't come out - eh?'

'Like enough. Yeah, it is some kind of fever.'

'I'll let a little more of 'er blood, if she's took that way again,' said Sikes.

Fagin nodded an expressive approval of this suggested treatment. 'Nothing that will trouble the doctor though, remember that Bill. No need for such a talented housebreaker as you to go the way of so many others, just because a woman doesn't know how to behave, and won't be trained.'

'She was hanging about me all day and night when I was on my back with the fever; and you, like a blackhearted wolf as you are, kept yourself aloof,' said Sikes. 'We was poor too, all the time, and I think, one way or other, it's worried and fretted her; and being shut up here so long has made her restless - eh?'

'That's it, my dear,' replied the Jew in a whisper. 'Hush!'

As he uttered these words, the girl appeared and resumed her former seat. Her eyes were swollen and red; she held a hand over a raw red mark at her temple as she rocked herself to and fro; tossed her head; and, after a little time, burst out laughing.

'Why, now she's on the other tack!' exclaimed Sikes, turning a look of surprise at Fagin.

Fagin nodded to him to take no further notice; and, in a few minutes, the girl subsided. Whispering to Sikes that there was no fear of her relapsing, Fagin took up his hat and bade him good-night. He paused when he reached the room-door, and looking round, asked if somebody would light him down the dark stairs.

'Light him down will you, Nance,' said Sikes, who was filling his pipe. 'It's a pity he should break his neck, and disappoint the sight-seers. Show him a light.'

Nancy followed the old man downstairs, carrying a candle. When they reached the passage, he laid his finger on his lip, and drawing close to the girl, said, in a whisper. 'What is it, Nancy, dear?'

'What do you mean?' replied the girl, in a flat tone.

'The reason for all this,' replied Fagin. He pointed with his skinny fore-finger up the stairs. 'Since 'e is so hard with you (he's a brute, Nance, a brute-beast), why don't you....'

'Well?' said the girl, as Fagin paused, with his mouth almost touching her ear, and his eyes looking sideways into hers.

'Isn't that how you like us?' she asked, 'I can't leave 'im, y'know that. And isn't that how you trained me to be? I'll always be 'is, to the day I die, and dying will be a blessing.'

Fagin continued to look sideways at her, attempting to read something in the low light of the candle and the flat expressionlessness of her eyes.

'We'll talk of this again,' he said. 'You have a friend in me, Nance; a staunch friend. I have the means at hand, quiet and close. If you want revenge on those that treat you like a dog! He treats you worse than his Bull's-eye, for he humours him sometimes - come to me. I say, come to me. He is the mere hound of a day...'

'The hound of the day....' she repeated. She had been looking glassily into the darkness, but she suddenly turned her face and looked at Fagin, so that he saw the deep dejected fatigue in her face. 'You know that isn't so,' she continued, then she mimicked his mode of speech by adding, '...my dear!'

'But you know me of old, Nance.'

'I know you too well, and thanks for everything you've done.' replied the girl, without manifesting the least emotion, nor did she betray the sarcasm she intended in the sound of her voice. 'Good-night.'

She shrank away as Fagin offered to lay his hand on hers, but she said good-night again, in a steady voice, and, answered his parting look with a nod, as though she had come back to her senses. She closed the door.

Fagin walked home, intent upon the thoughts that were working within his brain. He conceived the idea - not from what had just passed though that had tended to confirm him, but slowly and by degrees - that Nancy, wearied of the housebreaker's brutality, had conceived an attachment for someone new. Her altered manner, her absences from home alone, her comparative indifference to the interests of the gang for which she had once been so zealous. They all favoured his supposition, and rendered it, to him at least, almost a matter of certainty. Since he took it that the object of this new liking was not among his current myrmidons, he would be a valuable acquisition with such an assistant as Nancy, and must (thus Fagin argued) be secured without delay.

There was another, and a darker object, to be gained. Sikes knew too much, and his persistent ruffian taunts had always galled Fagin though he kept those wounds hidden. The girl must know well, that if she shook him off, she could never be safe from his fury, and that it would be surely brought - by maiming of limbs, or perhaps the loss of life - on the object of her new fancy.

'With a little persuasion,' thought Fagin, 'she would surely consent to poison him! Women have done such things, and worse, to secure their object before. Then the dangerous villain: the man upon which I depend for my liberty - for he knows too much of my dealings - and the man I hate, gone; with another secured in his place; and my influence over the girl unlimited, with my knowledge of this crime to back it.'

These things passed through Fagin's mind during the short time he sat alone in the housebreaker's room; and with them in his thoughts, he had taken the opportunity, of sounding out the girl in the hints he threw out at his parting. There was no expression of surprise by her, no assumption of an inability to understand his meaning. The girl clearly comprehended it. Her glance at parting showed that. It was all in her looks; any denial by words were inconsequential.

But perhaps she would recoil from a plot to take the life of Sikes, and that was his chief end. Such brains as Fagin's are fertile in expedients. If he laid a watch upon her, he reasoned, to discover the identity of her new attachment, and if he then threatened to reveal it to Sikes (of whom she stood, through persistent brutal practice, in no common fear) unless she entered into his designs, could he not secure her compliance?

He went on his way: busying his bony hands in the folds of his tattered garment, which he wrenched tightly in his grasp.

Oliver Twist, while in the care of Rose Maylie's family had the good fortune to see in the streets of that teeming metropolis, by perfect chance, his former protector, Mr. Brownlow, he who had taken him from the court after Oliver had been arrested. Miss Maylie established contact with him, and passed on, in confidence, as she had promised, the intelligence that Nancy had brought to her. Together they determined to keep an appointment with the young woman at London Bridge. Upon their first venture to meet her, Nancy had been unable to keep the informal appointment. The following week they make another attempt.

Unknown to Nancy, Fagin had kept to his own plan, to have all her movements followed and watched. Fagin engaged a young man for the task, whom he had tutored since his youngest years, named Noah Claypole.

The church clocks chimed three quarters past eleven. A mist hung over the river, deepening the red glare of the fires that burnt upon the small craft moored off the different wharfs, and rendering darker and more indistinct the murky buildings on the banks. The old smoke-stained storehouses on either side, rose heavy and dull from the dense mass of roofs and gables, and frowned sternly upon water too black to reflect even their lumbering shapes. The tower of old Saint Saviour's Church, and the spire of Saint Magnus, so long the giant-warders of the ancient bridge, were scarcely visible in the gloom; but the forest of shipping masts below the bridge, and the scattered spires of churches above, were nearly all hidden from sight.

Two figures emerged on to London Bridge. One, advanced with a swift and rapid step, was that of a woman who looked eagerly about her; the other figure was of a man, who slunk along in the deepest shadow he could find, and, while he kept at some distance, he maintained his pace to hers: stopping when she stopped: and as she moved again, moving stealthily on: but never allowing himself to gain upon her footsteps. Thus, they crossed the bridge, from the Middlesex to the Surrey shore, when the woman turned back. The movement was sudden; but he who watched her was not thrown off by it; for, he crossed over the road and allowed her to pass while he stood on the opposite pavement. When she was about the same distance in advance as she had been before, he continued to follow her again. At nearly the centre of the bridge, she stopped. The man stopped too. The girl took a few restless turns to-and-fro - closely watched by her hidden observer - when the heavy bell of St. Paul's tolled midnight and it's deep sound throbbed through the dense river mist and, though muffled, all across the crowded city.

The palace, the night-cellar, the jail, the madhouse: the chambers of birth and death, of health and sickness, the rigid face of the corpse and the calm sleep of the child: midnight was upon them all.

The hour had not struck more than two minutes, when a young lady, accompanied by a grey-haired gentleman, alighted from a hackney-carriage, the man dismissed the vehicle, and having scarcely set foot upon the pavement, the young girl who was being watched started forward towards them. They walked on, looking about them with the air of persons with only a slight expectation that their object would be realised, when they were joined by young woman. They halted with an exclamation of surprise, but suppressed it immediately; for a man in the garments of a countryman came close up and brushed against them in the mist at that moment.

'Not here,' said Nancy hurriedly, 'I'm afraid to speak to you here. Come - out of the public way - down the steps, there!' She indicated that she wished to proceed to the steps on the Surrey bank, and on the same side of the bridge as Saint Saviour's Church, where they form a landing-stairs from the river.

The countryman, having kept nearby but part obscured by the mist, looked to this spot, and, viewing the spot for a moment, rushed unobserved toward it and began to descend the steps.

These stairs are a part of the bridge and consist of three flights. Just below the end of the second, the stone wall on the left ends and, at this point, the lower steps widen: so that a person turning that angle of the wall, is unseen by any others on the stairs who chance to be above him. The countryman looked round when he reached this point; and as there seemed no better place to conceal himself - since the tide was out there was plenty of room - he slipped aside and waited: certain that they would come no lower, and that even if he could not hear what was said, he could follow them again, with safety.

The spy was eager to discover the motives for this meeting, so different from that which he had been led to expect. He heard the sound of footsteps, and then their voices very close-by. He drew himself upright against the wall, and, scarcely breathing, listened.

'This is far enough,' said a voice, that of the gentleman. 'I will not suffer the young lady to go farther. Many people would have distrusted you too much to have come even so far, but you see I am willing to humour you.'

'To humour me!' the voice of the girl said. 'You're considerate, indeed, sir. To humour me!'

'Please,' said another voice, the voice of a young lady, not the one whom Fagin had set him to watch. It was a very fine and sweet voice, 'for the help she offers, do not antagonise her.'

'Still,' began the gentleman, 'there are those that would, in such a dense mist, have for their purpose the intention to...'

There was the sound of light footsteps suddenly walking away.

The gentleman stopped talking.

'Please, I beg you,' said the very fine and sweet voice, now in an imploring tone. It spoke quite loudly, to be heard by the other woman, he that he had been set to watch, who was evidently walking away.

The sound of her footsteps stopped; he heard them scrape upon the pavement, then the sound of the person turning about, and slowly returning.

'Speak to her kindly,' continued the young lady. 'She needs it.'

'Why would you not have me speak to you above where it is light, and people are stirring,' said the gentleman in a kinder tone, 'instead of bringing us to this dismal hole?'

'I am afraid to speak to you there,' replied Nancy, with a tremble of anxiety in her voice. 'I don't know why it is, but I have such a fear and dread upon me to-night that I can hardly stand.'

'A fear of what?' asked the gentleman, who now seemed to pity her.

'I scarcely know,' replied the girl. 'I wish I did. Horrible thoughts of blood and death. I have burned, this day, as if I was on fire. I was attempting to read a book tonight, to wile the time - I can read a little, you see - hoping I would be able to get out to make this meeting, and the same things came into the print.'

'It is only your imagination playing with you,' said the gentleman, soothing her.

'No,' replied the girl in a hoarse voice. 'I'll swear I saw the words "death" and "coffin" written in every page of the book.'

There was something so uncommon in her manner, that the flesh of the concealed spy crept as he heard the girl utter these words, and the blood chilled within him, for he knew the possible outcome, once he reported this meeting to Fagin.

The girl continued, 'Your haughty religious people would have held their heads up to see me as I am to-night, and preached of flames and vengeance,' the girl said. 'Oh, lady, why ar'n't those who claim to be God's own folks as gentle and as kind to poor wretches as you are; you, who has youth and beauty, and all that such as I have lost?'

'Ah!' said the gentleman. 'A Turk turns his face, after washing it, to the East, when he says his prayers; these good people, after giving their faces such a rub as to take the smiles off, turn to the darkest side of Heaven. Between the Mussulman and the Pharisee, commend me to the first!'

These words appeared to be addressed to the young lady. The gentleman then addressed himself to Nancy. 'You were not here last Sunday night,' he said.

'I couldn't come,' replied Nancy; 'I was kept in by force.'

'By whom?'

'Him that I told the young lady of.'

'You were not suspected I hope?' asked the old gentleman.

'No,' replied the girl, shaking her head. 'It's not very easy for me to leave him unless he knows why; I couldn't give him a drink of laudanum before I came away, like I did when I came to see the lady before.'

'Did he awake before you returned?' inquired the young lady.

'No; luckily not. Neither he nor any of them suspect me.'

'Good,' said the gentleman. 'Now listen to me.'

'I am ready,' replied the girl, as he paused.

'This young lady,' the gentleman began, 'has communicated to me what you told her nearly a fortnight since. I confess that I had doubts, at first, whether you were to be relied upon, but now I firmly believe you. I repeat, I firmly believe it. To prove to you that I trust you, I tell you without reserve, that we propose to extort the secret, whatever it may be, from this man Monks. But if - if....' said the gentleman, 'he cannot be secured, or, cannot be acted upon as we wish, you must deliver up the Jew.'

'Fagin!' said the girl, and she recoiled. 'I will not do it! I will never do it!' replied the girl. 'Devil that he is, and worse than devil as he has been to me, I will never do that.'

'You will not?' said the gentleman in a tone of mild acceptance, and seemed fully prepared for this answer.

'Never!' returned the girl.

'Would you tell me why?'

'One reason alone,' replied the girl firmly, 'the lady knows it and will stand by me, I know she will, for I have her promise. And for this other reason; bad life as he has led, I have led as bad a life too. There are many of us who have kept the same course together, and I'll not turn upon them, for any of them might have turned upon me at any time, but they did not, bad as they are.'

'I understand,' said the gentleman, quickly, as if this had been the point he had been aiming to attain; 'then put Monks into my hands, and leave him to me to deal with.'

'What if he turns against the others?'

'I promise you that even if the truth is forced from him, the matter will rest with the information he will divulge about Oliver, and no more than that; and if the truth is elicited about the others, they shall go free. We are interested in what we can get from Monks about Oliver, only.'

'And if the truth is not got from him?' suggested the girl.

'Then,' pursued the gentleman, 'this Fagin shall not be brought to justice without your consent.'

'Have I the lady's promise for that?' asked the girl.

'You have,' replied Rose. 'My faithful pledge.'

'Monks would never learn how you knew about him?' said the girl, after a short pause.

'Never,' replied the gentleman. 'Information would be brought to bear upon him in such a way that he could never guess. He would be told that I had engaged an investigator, who had, by undisclosed means, discovered him, and his plot.'

'I have been a liar, and among liars from a little child,' said the girl after another interval of silence, 'so that I can scarcely know a spoken truth, but I will take your word.'

She proceeded in a voice so low that it was difficult for the spy to discover the purport of what she said, to describe, by name and situation, the public-house. She spoke haltingly, as though the gentleman were making hasty notes of the information. She explained the localities of the place, and various other details to facilitate an interception.

'He is tall,' the girl said, suddenly talking louder again, 'and strongly made, but not stout; he has a lurking walk; and as he walks, he constantly looks over his shoulder, first on one side, and then the other. His eyes are sunk in his head so much deeper than any other man's, that you might almost tell him by that alone. His face is dark, like his hair and eyes; and, although he can't be more than and twenty-six or eight, is withered and haggard. Part of this,' said the girl, 'I have drawn from people at the house I tell you of, for I have only seen him twice, and both times he was covered in a large cloak. Upon his throat: so high that you can see a part of it below his neckerchief when he turns his face: there is....'

'A broad red mark, like a burn or scald, perhaps even a rope burn?' cried the gentleman.

'You know him!' said the girl.

The young lady uttered a cry of surprise, and for a few moments they were so still that the listener could distinctly hear them breathe.

'I think I do,' said the gentleman, breaking the silence. 'I should by your description. We shall see. Many people are much like each other. It may not be the same.' He expressed himself with assumed carelessness, and must have taken a step or two nearer to the spy, as the latter could tell from the distinctness with which he heard him mutter, 'It must be!'

'You have given us most valuable assistance, young woman, and I wish you to be the better for it. What can I do to serve you?'

'Nothing,' replied Nancy.

'Miss Maylie told me that you refused her aid when you visited her. You will not persist in saying that,' replied the gentleman, with a voice and emphasis of kindness that would have touched even a much harder and more obdurate heart. 'Think on this. Kindness must prompt kindness, help and aid prompts help and aid in turn. You have offered us kindness and aid, we must reciprocate, and wish to do so, and to do so freely, not as obligation. Please tell me what I can do for you.'

'Nothing, sir,' rejoined the girl, suddenly weeping. 'You can do nothing to help me. Indeed, I am past all hope.'

'You put yourself beyond hope, I suspect,' said the gentleman. 'The past has been a dreary waste for you, and has wasted you, youthful energies have been mis-spent, and priceless treasures have been lavished and squandered; as it is bestowed once, so it is never granted again. For the future, though, you may still hope, surely. I do not say that it is in our power to offer you peace of mind, for that must come as you seek it; but for a quiet asylum, either in England, or, if you fear to remain here, across the Channel, it is both within our ability but our most anxious wish to secure this for you. Before this river wakes, you could be on any ship leaving this port, bound for safety beyond the knowledge and reach of your associates, and leave an absence of all trace behind, as if you had disappeared from the earth. Come! I would not have you go back to your old companions, or take one look at any old haunt, or breathe the air there, which is pestilence to you. Quit them, I plead with you, there is still time and opportunity!'

There was a pause.

'She will be persuaded, this time; I am sure' the young lady whispered. 'She hesitates.'

'No sir,' replied the girl, after a short struggle. 'I am chained to my old life. I loathe and hate it, but I cannot leave it. I have gone too far along this path to turn back now. Yet, I know, this fear comes over me again. Some time ago, I should have laughed it off. But, now,' she said, looking round, 'I must go home. He expects me, and I must be there.'

'Home?' queried the young lady, with great stress upon the word. 'Surely by your own admission, it is a loathed place, one that you are chained too. Such a place is a prison, it may be many things, but not a home. Never a home.'

'Home, lady,' replied the girl. 'It is such a place as I have made for myself with the work of my whole life...'

'Not *your* life,' interrupted the gentleman, 'it is the life that was forced upon you. It has been your life, *to date*, but not your whole life. You are young, there is so much of life ahead of you. Release your grip upon your old life and reach out for this other. We hold it out to you.'

'No. For me , it is home. Let us not argue the issue again. Let us part before I am watched or seen. Go! If I have done you service, all I ask is, that you leave me, and let me go my way.'

'We compromise her safety, perhaps, by staying here,' said the gentleman, with a sigh. 'We may have detained her longer than is safe already. I would prefer that you came away with us, but I see you will not be persuaded.'

'What, though, can be the end for this poor woman!' the sweet voiced young lady asked in a passion.

'It is this!' the girl said, calmly. 'Look! Look at the dark water. How many times do you read of those who leap in, and leave no living thing to be cared for, nor who bewails them. Old Father Thames is a friend to many who are friendless or hopeless. It may be years, it may be months, but I shall come to that.'

'Do not speak of this,' replied the young lady, giving herself entirely up to sobbing.

'It will never reach your ears!' replied the girl. 'But don't we all end in silence? There are many unknown people who wash up on this shore.'

'If you should think on our offer, we can still be contacted at the place you visited before, we will leave a message that you are to be admitted immediately, without question or argument,' the gentleman said.

'Take this purse,' the young lady said through her sobs. 'Take it, that you may have some resource in an hour of need, take it for my sake.'

'No!' replied the girl with resolution. 'I have not done this for money. Everything I have done in my life has been mercenary. I wish this action to be offered, by me, with no reward other than in the deed. I wish that it has been of service to you, to recover young Oliver. For, in him, I see a life he can have, that I never could. Good-night then, good-night!'

'Wait!' replied the gentleman. 'There are few that can live without money.' His voice was quieter now. 'There are fewer people, still, who do not have to acquire it, toil for if, think of it, desire it, dream of it, worry about it; and those that do not can only do so because someone, whether family, relation, or antecedent has freed them of the necessary burden. We must all trade, whether it be our time, or talents, or skills - in whatever form they take - and if not by those mean, then merely in the strength of our arms or by our bodily form.'

'Money is the salve for every pain, isn't it? - if only that were true my life would be no pain at all! I have never found it to be so. And yet - I would have you give me something of your own, that you have worn: I should like to have something.'

'A token?'

'Yes - but no, no! Not of great value. Please, no, not your ring - something like your gloves, or a handkerchief - anything I can keep, as having belonged to you. There, that's it. These I will wear. God bless you, lady. Stay here please, while I go. So we are not to be seen emerging together.'

The grave agitation of the girl, and her fear of being discovered, which would subject her to ever greater ill-usage and violence, was demonstrated by the tremble in her voice.

'Good-night!' said the girl.

'Good-night,' the two others said together.

'And thank you,' added the young lady. So unusual to her ears were those two words, 'thank you', that the other woman was startled at hearing them addressed to her. The other voice continued to come to her through the fog. 'May God reserve a place for those that overcome their mean circumstances and their hopelessness, to help, as you have done, a child who might have otherwise been forced to follow a path like yours; who has loathed it, but who has become dependent upon it as certainly as if chains had locked you to your fate. With this kindness you have overcome all the mean circumstances that made you. I wish that I could alleviate the treatment you were ever subjected to.'

The spy had noted that the footsteps had stopped as this was said, once concluded the footsteps sounded again as the wretched girl walked away. Then the lady called after her in a loud whisper.

'Wait! You know my name, I do not know yours. If nothing else, would you tell me that, so I may thank you by name?'

The footsteps stopped for a few moments. All was silent, before she started to walk rapidly away again. She stopped, and in a loud whisper she gave her name, 'Nancy. My name is Nancy... Nancy Porter.'

'Thank-you,' the young lady returned; those two simple words, again, often spoken in the glibbest manner were, here, spoken and laden with the sincerest gratitude. 'Thank-you, Nancy,' the young lady continued before collapsing into quiet sobbing. The spy could see her slight frame leaning in toward the gentleman for comfort. Otherwise, on that misty river bank, the voices ceased. The figure of the girl soon afterwards appeared passing under a lamp on the bridge, and the young lady and her companion waited a minute as requested, and then slowly followed. They stopped at the summit of the steps.

'Hark!' cried the young lady, listening. 'Did she call! I thought I heard her voice.'

'No, my love,' replied Mr Brownlow. Rose Maylie seemed minded to linger, but the old gentleman took her arm and led her, with gentle force, away. As they emerged into the pale light of the gas lamp the young lady sank down to sit on one of the stone steps, and vented the anguish of her heart, fully, in the bitterest tears. The gentleman bowed over her, helping her back to her feet, and she could only walk away with his support, with feeble and tottering steps.

The astonished listener had remained, watching, motionless at his post until the two others disappeared into the mist. He slunk from his hiding-place, stealthily, always in the shade of the wall, all in the same manner as he had come. When he reached the top, Noah Claypole darted away at speed, and made for Fagin's house as fast as his legs would carry him.

It was nearly two hours before day-break; that time which in the autumn of the year, may be truly called the dead of night; when the streets are deserted and when even sounds appear to slumber, when profligacy and riot have staggered home to dream; it was at this still and silent hour, that Fagin sat watching in his old lair, with his face so distorted and pale, and eyes so blood-shot, that he looked less like a man, than like some hideous phantom, moist from the grave.

He sat crouching over a cold hearth, wrapped in an old torn coverlet, with his face turned towards a wasting candle that stood upon a table. His right hand was raised to his lips, and, absorbed in thought, he bit his long black nails.

Stretched upon a mattress on the floor, lay Noah Claypole, fast asleep. Towards him the old man busy elsewhere.

He was mortified to find that his scheme had no leverage, he felt bitter disappointment at the loss of his revenge on Sikes; and hatred for the girl that he had raised and trained and who had dared to palter with strangers; he distrusted the sincerity of her refusal to yield him up; he felt the fear of detection, and ruin - and, most of all, he felt the fear of hanging. A fierce and deadly rage was kindled within him. These were the thoughts he considered which, following close upon each other in a ceaseless whirl, shot through the brain of Fagin, as every evil thought and blackest purpose lay working within him.

He sat without changing his attitude, or appearing to take the smallest heed of time, until his quick ear seemed to be attracted by a footstep in the street.

'At last,' he muttered, wiping his dry and fevered mouth. 'At last! We'll have it all out now!'

'Wot now?' cried Sikes as he came in, having received a message to come to Fagin from one of his boys.

Fagin raised his right hand and shook his trembling forefinger in the air; but his passion was so great, that the power of speech was for the moment gone.

'Damme!' said Sikes, looking at him with alarm. 'He's gone mad.'

'No,' replied Fagin, finding his voice. 'You're not the person, Bill. I've no - no fault to find with you.'

'Oh? You haven't?' said Sikes, looking at him, and ostentatiously passing a pistol into a more convenient pocket.

'You must look to others, those that you know,' said Fagin.

'Well, that's lucky - for one of us. Which one that is, don't matter.'

'What I've got that to tell you, Bill,' said Fagin, drawing his chair near.

'Aye?' returned the robber. 'Tell away! And look sharp.' Sikes eyes narrowed, as he looked with perplexity into Fagin's face, he clenched Fagin's coat lapel in his huge hand and shook him soundly. 'Speak, will you!' he demanded; 'Open your mouth and say wot you've got to say in plain words. Out with it, you old cur! Out with it!'

'Suppose that lad that's laying there....' Fagin began. Sikes turned round to where Noah Claypole was sleeping, as if he had not previously observed him. 'Well!' he continued, 'suppose that lad was to peach - first seeking out the right folks for the purpose, and then having a meeting with 'em to paint our likenesses, describe every mark that they might know us by, and the crib where we might be easily found. Suppose he was to do this, and more besides, of his own fancy; not grabbed, trapped, tried, earwigged by the parson, and brought to it on bread and water, but of his own fancy and infamy; stealing out at nights to find those who are most interested against us, and peaching to them. Do you hear me?' Fagin said, his eyes flashing with rage. 'Suppose he did all this, what then?'

'What then!' replied Sikes. 'I'd grind his skull under the heel of my boot into as many grains as there are hairs upon his head.'

'What if I did it!' Fagin continued, his voice becoming peculiarly quieter as his rage vented itself. 'I, that knows so much, and could hang so many besides myself!'

'I don't know,' replied Sikes, clenching his teeth and turning white at the suggestion. 'I'd do something in the jail that 'ud get me put in irons; and if I was tried along with you, I'd fall upon you in the open court, and beat your brains out afore the people. I should have such strength,' muttered the robber, poising his brawny arm, 'that I could smash your head as if a loaded waggon had gone over it.'

Fagin made no answer, but bending over the sleeper again, hauled him into a sitting posture. Noah rubbed his eyes, and, giving a heavy yawn, looked sleepily about him.

'Tell me that again - once again, just for him to hear,' said Fagin, pointing to Sikes.

'Tell yer what?' asked the sleepy Noah, shaking himself pettishly.

'That about - Nancy,' said Fagin, clutching Sikes by the wrist, as if to prevent his leaving the house before he had heard enough. 'You followed her, right?'

'Yes.'

'To London Bridge?'

'Yes.'

'Where she met two people.'

'So she did.'

'A gentleman and a lady that she had gone to of her own accord, who asked her to give up her pals, and Monks first, which she did - she described him in detail, which she did - and to tell her what house it was that we meet at, which she did - and where it could be best watched from, which she did - and what time the people went there, which she did. She did all this. She told it all, every word without a threat - she did - did she not?' asked Fagin, to bring it all to Sikes attention.

'All right,' replied Noah, scratching his head. 'That's just what it was!'

'What did they say, about last Sunday?'

'About last Sunday!' replied Noah, considering. 'Why I told yer that before.'

'Again. Tell it again!' cried Fagin, tightening his grasp on Sikes.

'They asked her,' said Noah, who, as he grew more wakeful, seemed to have a dawning perception who Sikes was, 'they asked her....' He stopped talking, when he recommenced he simply said, 'I told you all this. You woke me, let me sleep.'

'Tell 'im!' Fagin said threateningly, drawing a blade from his coat. 'Tell 'im why she didn't come, last Sunday, as she had promised.'

'She said she couldn't.'

'Why - why?' insisted Fagin, 'Tell him that too.'

'Because she was forcibly kept at home by the man she had told them of before,' replied Noah.

'What more?' cried Fagin. 'Tell him that, tell him that too.'

'Why, that she couldn't very easily get out of doors unless he knew where she was going to,' said Noah; 'and so the first time she went to see the lady, she - ha! ha! - it could've made me laugh when she said it - she gave him laudanum to ensure 'e slept.'

Fagin looked at Sikes, watching the expression upon his face.

'Hell's fire!' cried Sikes as he turned away toward the door

Fagin grabbed at the housebreaker's coat, to hold him back.

'Let me go!' cried Sikes, flinging the old man from him, he rushed from the room, and darted, wildly and furiously, away.

'Bill, Bill!' cried Fagin, following him. 'A word. Only a word.'

The word would not have been exchanged, but the housebreaker was unable to open the door: on which he was expending fruitless oaths, when Fagin came panting up to him.

'Let me out,' said Sikes. 'Don't speak to me; it's not safe. I'll take it out on somebody, this instant, if you don't let me out!'

Fagin laid his hand upon the lock to stop Bill Sikes struggling with it. Before he drew it open he brought his lips up to Sikes left ear, 'Hear me speak a word before you go,' he whispered.

'Well?' replied the other.

'You won't be...'

'Yes?'

'You won't be *too* violent, Bill? Remember. Rule by fear, rule by fear, but don't take it too far. Be harsh, but not too much. Remember, the hangman is always ready with his noose.'

The day was breaking, and there was light enough for the men to see each other's faces now. Fagin drew his head back from whispering. They exchanged one brief glance; there was a fire in the eyes of both. But, being younger and stronger, the fire in the eyes of Bill Sikes flared as the graver danger.

'I mean,' said Fagin, showing that he felt all disguise was now useless, 'not *too* violent, for safety's sake. Be crafty, Bill, crafty, like; and not too bold.'

Sikes made no reply; but, pulling open the door, of which Fagin had turned the lock, he dashed into the silent streets. Without a pause, or moment's consideration; or raising his eyes to the sky, or lowering them to the ground, but looking straight ahead with savage resolution, he dashed on his headlong course, nor muttered, nor relaxed a muscle, until he reached his own door. He opened it, softly, with a key; strode up the stairs as lightly as his large frame would allow; entering his room, he turned and locked the door and pocketed the key in his waistcoat, then he slid the dead bolt across, and turned to draw back the curtain of the bed.

FATAL CONSEQUENCES; THE DREADFUL MURDER

The girl was lying, half-dressed, upon the bed. He roused her from her sleep with a violent shake, and she raised herself with a startled look. If he had cared to notice he would have seen the faint streaking of tears on her face. Without looking at Sikes she remembered the thoughts she had

had before she had slept, she had been thinking of the words the young lady and the old gentleman had said to her. Of the offer of a foreign asylum, and of hope. She smiled a very small smile as the last thought she had as she fell to sleep bounded back to her recollection; that old word, hope, was much like an entirely new word to her, it was full of meaning and possibilities.

'It is you, Bill!' said the girl, with an expression of pleasure at his return.

'It is,' was the reply. 'Get up.'

There was a candle burning, but the man hastily drew it from the candlestick, and hurled it under the grate. She watched him do it and frowned sleepily, but seeing the faint light of early day outside, the girl rose from the bed and drew on her skirt and short jacket; she glanced quickly at Bill Sikes as she tucked something she held in her hand, something light coloured, within the jacket, at the bosom, and she buttoned the jacket up quickly as she walked to the window to undraw the curtain.

'Let it be,' said Sikes. She turned instead to the table and laid a worn off-white cloth on the table-top. He sat down on a chair by the table and watched her bustle around the room through his narrow eyes. He rocked the chair back and forth on the two rear legs; all the while Fagin's revelation whirled in his mind. She set a place for him, that is, she put down a fork and a mug, and, still sleepily, she turned to attend to the fire and to heat a kettle for his morning tea.

'There's enough light in 'ere for wot I've got to do with you.'

'Bill?' the girl said, in a low voice of alarm, knowing the tone in his voice and what it presaged. She stopped and looked at him for the first time that morning.

'Why do you look at me like that?' she asked.

The robber remained sitting, regarding her, with dilated nostrils and heaving breast; then, he leapt from the chair and, grabbing her at the throat, he dragged her into the middle of the room

'Bill, Bill!' gasped the girl, wrestling against him with the strength that fear lends, 'I - I won't cry out - you know - I won't! But - hear me.'

'"Hear me," she says. I've heard just about as much as ever I'm going to hear from you.'

'I haven't done anything!' she screamed as loudly as his constricting fist upon her throat would allow. 'Speak to me, Bill' she pleaded, 'tell me what it is I've done!'

He let go of her throat but took hold of her hair and twisted her round so that her back was to his face, he put his other heavy hand upon her mouth. He leaned in toward her and placed his mouth close to her ear.

'Tell you what you've done?' he breathed in a low malevolent whisper, 'You know what you've done! You she-devil!' Then he sprang it on her, 'You were watched last night; every word you said was heard.'

The girl struggled and squirmed free from his hold. She would have her say. 'I didn't give up anyone from the gang, Bill...'

He lunged at her again, grabbed at her hair and twisted it around in his fist.

'You gave all the particulars, and our haunt...'

'Not of you, Bill. Not of here. I only gave up Monks, for what he would to do to the child.'

'The child! What is it about that boy? They were gentle-folk, I'm told. How much did you sell us out for?'

'It wasn't for money, Bill. It was just the child, to save him from what Monks wants to do. An' I came back, didn't I? If I had given you up, I would never have returned, surely?'

'*You peached*,' he said emphatically, and in those two words she sensed a finality of judgement in his voice. It was the voice that gave it away as much as the words; it had another quality. She knew Bill's violence all too well; it was usually careless, harsh but brief; sometimes he would slap her once, sometimes many times, sometimes he would grab her tightly and shake her roughly, sometimes he would punch her, to the body, sometimes to the head. In his tone now, she sensed another degree of rage; her action had not only roused his usual malevolence but an anger of another order, she was gripped by mortal fear; she had spoken the previous night of her violent end, but had not suspected that the time was to come so soon. So soon.

'Spare my life! Spare it, though it is worth little to me, or anyone. Please, spare me my life. It's all I have, I have little else. For the love of Heaven, Bill!' the girl pleaded, turning upon him and clinging to him, she hung ferociously onto him, pinning his arms by his side. She must keep herself attached to him, so that he exhausted himself and exhausted this rage. If only she could. She knew that if she should lose this grip she could not live.

'Bill! Dear Bill. Think of all I've done for you. Think of all I have given for you. You cannot have the heart. Think! Think! Would you kill me? You've threatened it enough before. Save yourself this crime; take the time to think on it. I will not loose my hold, you cannot throw me off.'

'I can't? Is that so?'

'Bill, Bill, for dear God's sake, for your own sake, and mine, stop! I have been true to you, always, upon my guilty soul I have!'

The man struggled violently, to release his arms; but the arms of the girl were clasped round his so closely, so that, struggle against her as he would, he could not tear his arms free.

'Bill,' cried the girl looking up into his face, 'the gentleman and the lady, they told me of a home in some foreign country where I could live in solitude and peace. Let me see it! Let me see them, and beg them to show the same mercy to you; let us both leave this place, and lead better lives, and forget how we have ever had to live, and never see this place again, or see each other more. They're not vindictive, they won't prosecute, they promised me that!'

'A gentleman and a lady! Their promises don't mean anything to *us*! How long have you lived in the streets, girl!'

'They only wanted information about Oliver! That's all! It's never too late to repent. They told me so - I feel it now - but we must have time - a little... time. Time!' The last few words came out as somewhere between a cry and a gasp.

'If I'm to be hanged I'll take the one that snitched on me before I go,' he snarled, his greater strength beginning to tell in their struggle.

'Then don't kill me, and let us get away from here. I'll go ahead - to the people - I met - I'll get their - assurances....' The girls voice trailed off, she was becoming weaker by the moment, so great was his huge strength that she had to subdue. 'You can't wish to be without me, Bill,' she suddenly screamed. 'You can't! You can't!

'I don't care to think that I've been with you...'

'Then kill me if you must, for I don't wish to be without you...'

The housebreaker freed one arm, and plunged that arm into his overcoat and grasped his pistol. The certainty of immediate detection if he fired, flashed across his mind even in the midst of his fury. And it was his fury that gave him the inevitable strength to overcome the extra strength of her mortal fear, for he was able to wrest her last grip from his body. Having got his arm loosened from her, he flung her - more by momentum as by his greater power - across the room, but she grabbed at his clothing, at his overcoat and clung on. Yet in this action she aided his intention, holding herself at such close quarters by her grip on his clothes, she held herself close to him, as though in an embrace, her head laid against his breast; as she raised her head to look up at him, to plead anew; he beat down with the pistol handle twice with all the force he could summon, upon the upturned head.

The stunning might of the blows caused her to stagger, but still she launched herself at the door and clung to the handle as she tried to turn it, to escape from the room. Even if it had not been locked and bolted she had not the strength to turn it. She slumped to the floor, nearly blinded with the blood that flowed from the deep gashes above her hairline - yet she did not see, nor perceive it as her own blood, only as a strange moistness around her head. She drew her sleeved forearm across her head where the gash was, and looked astonished at the blood smeared on her forearm, cuff and sleeve.

She raised herself, with difficulty, onto her knees, and drew something from out of her clothing, something that had been held close to her body, at her bosom - cream coloured kid-gloves, embroidered at the cuff with the letters R.M.; Rose Maylie's gloves, the item that Nancy had requested earlier that night and had been given - she clutched them in her folded hands.

'What have you got there,' Sikes demanded to the near insensible girl. He grabbed the gloves from her hands.

'No!' the girl, who had said she would not scream, now screamed out. 'Let me have them back!'

He put the flat of his hand upon her face and casually pushed her over while he held the gloves in the other and examined them momentarily; he shrugged and threw them to the floor. Nancy used the little strength remaining to her to slump upon her elbows and reach across the floor to take them back into her hands. She held the soft leather to her cheek, and was outraged to see the blood, her blood, smeared across them.

She clasped the bloodied gloves in her bloodied hands and turned her bloodied head towards the Heavens, as much as her feeble strength could allow her to hold herself up. She breathed a prayer for mercy; it was a long forgotten prayer, from her brief attendance at a Sunday School when aged five or six years of age, but now, suddenly, she remembered it. As her head slumped down again she repeated it over and over.

Sikes grabbed her by the hair again to drag her back to the middle of the room, there was no fight left in her, nor much breath, she hung limply from his grip so that he could not move her; he had to adjust his grasp to hold on to her clothes instead, to drag her. He deposited her in a heap on the rug in the middle of the room. He staggered back and seized a heavy club that was leaning against the wall by the fire. She heard his movements and raised her head once more, to look at him. She was defeated.

He raised the club; he saw her eyes looking up at him; being near insensibility, and bloodied as she was, and he, being a practised defiler of innocence in his earlier youth, before he had taken up with Nancy, he knew the look. She had the appearance of an innocent.

'Bill?' she said in a feeble undertone, 'It is you?'

He brought the club down on her with enormous force and struck her, and struck her, and struck her...

Of all dreadful deeds that, under cover of darkness, had ever been committed within London's wide bounds, that, surely, was the worst. The sun - the bright sun, that brings, not light alone, but new life, and hope, and freshness to man - could have hidden itself again, on the night side of the earth, if it were sensible to what it would illuminate, for the shame of it; being entirely insensible, it burst upon the crowded city in clear and radiant glory. Whether it was through costly-coloured glass or a paper-mended window, such as this room that Bill Sikes and Nancy Porter shared, or upon a cathedral dome or into a rotten crevice, the sun sheds its rays equally, without indulgence to any one over any other. It lighted the room where the woman lay.

Such a sight as that could only ever be ghastly, even in the dull morning before dawn; but what was it now, in all that brilliant light! The light would stream in, although Sikes tried to shut it out. He had removed his coat and hung it over the window to snuff out all that newly dawned - revealing - daylight that lighted upon her brazen body slumped upon the floor.

He had upended the chair as he had flown at her in his violence, he stooped to put it the right way up and slumped upon it and sat silently, motionlessly; and remained sitting, so that he had not moved, nor could he discover the strength within his broad frame to move. Then there had been a moan from her and a motion of the hand; in his horror, more than his diminishing rage, he had leapt at her prostrate figure and struck, and struck, and struck her again with the club.

It was the eyes, though. The eyes that stared sightlessly - at *him.*

He picked up two opposite corners of the rug and threw them over the battered figure; but he then found that it was worse to *imagine* the eyes than to see them glaring up at him; to imagine them looking at him - and seeing, again, the look in her eyes at the instant that he had first struck her with the pistol butt, and then the club; the look in them as she waned under the violence of his murderous assault - it was worse having them covered than it was to see them glaring sightlessly up at him; glaring as if they were watching the reflection of the light off the table-cloth that caused the spatter of blood on the ceiling to quiver and dance with the reflected sunlight upon it. So, he had plucked the rug off again. There was the body - mere sparkless flesh and stilled blood; that was all, and no more than that - but *such* flesh, and *so much* blood had been freed from the flesh by his insensate brutish assault.

He got up and kindled the fire, and thrust the tool of his attack, the club, to burn it and warm the room and bring a shadowed and mute light into it.

He saw, then, that there were strands of her hair upon the end of the club, straggling there so much like a cutting given by a newly-discovered love as a remembrance of their declaration of their love, those few strands blazed in an instant in the burgeoning flame and shrunk down into a bright cinder, and then, caught by the air, they whirled up the chimney. Even that frightened him, sturdy as he was; he used his booted foot to shove the club into the coals till it was so deeply consumed by the flame that it became embers and broke, then he piled coals upon it to burn it further away, to have it smoulder into the blackened soul that burnt embers resemble, and then on down to ashes.

How long did he remain with Nancy's body heaped in the centre of that room ? He did not know.

He removed his overcoat from the window and washed himself, and rubbed his clothes; but there were spots that would not be removed. He took a blade and scraped away at the blackening spots, to reduce the mark, then he cut other pieces out, those that could not be reduced by either water or blade, and burnt them in the fireplace too. And how all those other stains were dispersed about the room! Upon the sloping ceiling, upon the walls, upon the door and the door-handle, upon the bed clothes, upon a change of clothes that Nancy had hung upon a hook on the door, upon the table top where she had spread the cloth, even on the mug that she had set down on the table-top had a spatter of blood across it. The very feet of the dog were bloody too, having followed it's owner as he had moved around the room, so it had padded through the blood. It's mouth was bloodied, it seemed it had lapped upon the blood, it being thirsty, while Sikes had sat senselessly after the attack.

All this time he never once turned his back upon the corpse for a moment, lest she should once more moan and move a hand, or rise again. He moved, backward, towards the door, dragging the dog with him around the pooled blood, lest he should soil his feet anew and carry the evidence of the crime from the concealing interior out into the open streets.

He shut the door softly behind him, locked it, took the key, and left the house. Outside, he glanced at the window. There was the curtain still drawn, which she would have opened, perhaps he should have drawn it to show to any glance upward that the inhabitants were up and about - but would anyone notice, or care? He knew, God, how he knew, how the sun would be pouring through that thin and worn veil of cloth they used as a curtain - upon the very spot where she lay! But the sun was moving upon its daily track toward the zenith, it would move around soon enough and that body would soon lie again in shadow.

The glance was instantaneous. It was a relief to have got free of the room. Being out upon the common thoroughfare of the city he felt a momentary lifting of his spirits. He whistled to the dog, and walked away.

THE FLIGHT OF SIKES; THE MURDERER ATTEMPTS ESCAPE

He went through Islington; strode up the hill at Highgate; turned down to Highgate Hill; he was as unsteady of purpose and uncertain where to go as he had been vigorous and certain in his assault. He struck off to the right, almost as soon as he began to descend the hill; and taking the foot-path across the fields, skirted Caen Wood, and so came on Hampstead Heath. Crossing the hollow by the Vale of Heath, he mounted the opposite bank, and crossing the road which joins the villages of Hampstead and Highgate, made along the heath to the fields at the North End, in one of these fields he laid himself down under a hedge, and slept.

Soon he was up again, and away, not into the country, but back towards London by the high-road - then back again - then over another part of the same ground - then wandering up and down fields, following paths any which way, and starting up to make for some other spot, and do the same, and to always ramble on.

Where could he go, that was near and not too public, to get some meat and drink? Hendon. That was a good place, not far off, and out of most people's way. He directed his steps there, sometimes running, and sometimes, with a strange perversity, loitering, or stopping. But when he got there, all the people he met - the very children at the doors - seemed to look upon him with suspicion. Back he turned again, without the courage to purchase bit of food or a drop, though he had tasted no food for hours; and once more he lingered on the Heath, still uncertain where to go until morning and noon had passed, and the day was on the wane. Still he rambled up and down, and round and round. At last he got away, making a course for Hatfield.

It was nine o'clock at night, when the man, tired out (and the dog, limping and lame from the unaccustomed exercise) turned down the hill by the church of the village, and plodding along the street, crept into a public-house, whose scanty light had guided them. There was a fire in the tap-room, and some country-labourers were drinking around it. They made room for the stranger, but he sat down in the furthest corner, and ate and drank apart from them, while he cast a cut-off of meatless fat to his dog from time to time. The robber, after paying his reckoning, sat silent and unnoticed in his corner, and had almost dropped asleep, when he was half wakened by the noisy entrance of a newcomer. This was an antic fellow, half pedlar and half mountebank, who travelled on foot to vend hones, strops, razors, harness-paste, washballs, medicine for dogs and horses, cheap perfumery, cosmetics, and such-like wares, which he carried in a case slung to his back.

His entrance was the signal for various homely jokes with the countrymen, which did not slacken until he had made his supper, and opened his box of treasures, when he ingeniously contrived to unite business with amusement.

'And what be that?' asked a grinning country man, pointing to some composition-cakes in one corner.

'This,' said the fellow, 'this is the infallible and invaluable composition for removing all sorts of stain, rust, dirt, mildew, spick, speck, spot, or spatter, from silk, satin, linen, cambric, cloth, crape, stuff, carpet, merino, muslin, or any woollen stuff. Wine-stains, fruit-stains, beer-stains, water-stains, paint-stains, pitch-stains, all stains, all come out at one rub with this infallible and invaluable composition. If a lady stains her honour, she has only need to swallow one cake and she's cured at once - for it's poison. It's quite as satisfactory as a pistol-bullet for any gentleman who has also lost his, whether it be in fisticuffs, or cards, or other wager, thought this is a great deal nastier in the flavour, so there is more credit in taking it. One penny a square. With all these virtues, one penny a square! Ha! See!' he added, seeing Sikes hat upon a chair next to him, 'Here is a stain upon the hat of a gentleman in this company, that I'll take clean out, before he can order me a pint of ale.'

'Hah!' cried Sikes starting up. 'Give that back to me.'

'It'll take that stain clean out, sir,' replied the man, winking to the company, 'Gentlemen, observe the stain upon this gentleman's hat, no wider than a shilling, but thicker than a half-crown....'

The man got no further, for Sikes raged at him, 'I'll keep the stain... for sentimental reasons,' then he added a hideous imprecation and overturned the table. He tore the hat back from the peddler and burst out of the public house.

Yet it was with the same perversity of irresolution of before that the murderer, despite himself, turned back toward the town; when he recognised the mail from London, and saw that it was standing at the little post-office. He crossed over, and listened.

The guard was standing at the door, waiting for the letter-bag.

'Now, look alive in there, will you.' said the guard. 'Damn that 'ere bag, it warn't ready night afore last; this won't do!'

'Anything new up in town, Ben?' the man at the post-office asked.

'No, nothing that I knows on,' replied the man, pulling on his gloves. 'Corn's up a little. I heard talk of a murder, down Spitalfields way.'

'That's true, a dreadful murder it was, so we hear. Quite battered. Dreadfully battered. Marked all over with the signs of the worst violence.'

'That so, sir?' rejoined the guard, touching his hat. 'Man or woman, pray?'

'A woman,' replied the gentleman.

'Damn that 'ere bag,' said the guard, uninterested in a common-or-garden sort of murder in Spitalfields; 'are you gone to sleep in there?'

'Coming!' cried the office keeper, running out.

'Coming,' growled the guard. 'Ah, and so's the young 'oman of property that's going to take a fancy to me, but I don't know when. All ri-ight!'

The horn sounded a few cheerful notes, and the coach was gone.

Sikes remained standing, apparently unmoved by what he had heard, and agitated by no stronger feeling than a doubt of where to go; he was entirely overcome with this strange listlessness, greater than ordinary physical tiredness, even though he had been walking all day. At some length he took the road which leads from Hatfield to St. Albans.

He went on into the solitude and darkness of the road, but as he travelled further from the city he felt a dread and awe creeping upon him which shook him. Every object, substance or shadow, still or moving, took the semblance of some fearful thing; he could trace the smallest outline of a shadow and, in the gloom, supply it with life. It was not the sight of things alone that caused him to shiver. The sound of her voice - pleading, crying out to him - sounded in the silent night, as certainly and surely as though she was writhing at his feet, still being subjected to his blows. Then his senses altered the scene in his mind once again, so that these fears were as nothing compared to the next that struck him; that the morning's ghastly figure was following at his heels. He could hear its garments rustling in the leaves, and every breath of wind came laden with that last low expiring moan. If he stopped walking, it did the same. If he ran, it followed - not running: that would have been a relief:, but like a corpse endowed with the mere machinery of life, it was borne on one slow melancholy wind that ever rose or fell.

At times, he turned with desperate determination, but the hair rose on his head, for it, the shadow, or shade, had turned as he had turned, so that it was always, always, behind him. All the while he has the sense the figure was there but always out of visible sight. He had never turned his back to it that morning, but now it was behind him - always behind. His blood pounded in his chest and at his temples, he sweated and shivered and his blood seemed chilled. He leaned his back against a walled bank, and felt at the firm stones, his fingers moved across the soft moss, and he sensed the damp smell of soil; and the shadow of the murdered girl stood above him, visibly out against the cold night-sky. He threw himself out again upon the road - and it was immediately at his back again. Then it was at his head, silent, and still - a living grave-stone, with its epitaph, not graven, but scrawled across it - in her blood.

Let no man talk of murderers escaping justice, and hint that Providence must be sleeping to allow this to happen. There were twenty score of violent deaths in every long minute of that agony of fear for Sikes. There was no rest, no escape, no refuge from it. It was always there. Always.

He passed a shed in a field and turned toward it for the shelter it offered. Before the door, were three tall poplar trees, which made it very dark within; and the wind moaned through those trees with a dismal wail. He felt, that having stopped, he could not walk on till daylight came. To think, that there could be another morning, another dawn with the bright lively sun rising, as it had done yesterday, but without her, and it would draw the sight of her body again from shadow. Yet had not that man at the post office said that the body had been discovered? He could not recall with any certitude.

He stretched himself close to the wall with fatigue laying deep in his limbs - only to undergo new torture. For now, a vision rose before him, as constant and terrible than that from which he had escaped. It was those widely staring eyes, so lustreless, that he had thought it better to bear the sight of them than to think upon them; they appeared in the midst of the darkness, they held the nature of light in themselves, but gave light to nothing. There were but two, but they were everywhere. When he shut out that sight, in its stead there came the sight of the room with every well-known object - some, indeed, that he would have forgotten, if he had gone over its contents from memory - he saw her few personal possessions, each in its accustomed place; her combs, most with broken teeth, and brushes with strands of her hair caught in the bristles, the shard of mirrored glass propped against the wall, a small silver coloured casket with her various small nik-naks within. Her well worn pair of boots, one with a broken heel. Her shawl over the bed stead. The cloth upon the table. The empty bird cage with the bent-in wires that had never held a captive bird. Her sole valuable possession, the small conical pale fuchsia drinking glass made of crystal, or so she had thought. And the body - the body too was in its place, and its eyes were as he saw them when he had left the room. He leapt up, despite his deep fatigue, and rushed into the field. The figure was immediately behind him again. He re-entered the shed, and shrunk down once more with his back to the side of the shed. The eyes were there again, before he had laid himself down.

He remained in such terror as none but he can know, every limb trembling, in a cold sweat, when suddenly there arose upon the night a sudden startling wind, the noise grew to a great pitch, the trees were flung about by its gusts. Springing to his feet, he rushed into the open air again. He was fleeing from the deed, the dead; and weeping beyond measure, he shouted out into the night til his voice failed him, yet still his face was twisted by his need to cry out; he was fleeing from memory, from himself; so it was that he plunged blindly along throughout the night. If only there were some refuge from both weariness and thought. She was always before him, behind him, above him; the dreadful consciousness of his crime was always about and within him. Hither and thither he dived about that night, till joyless, lifeless morning dawned again, and him thoroughly fatigued and sleepless.

He awoke. He found that he had, without being aware of it, slumped by the side of the road at some time in the drear grey early light, and slept briefly but deeply, an unrefreshing but dreamless sleep.

On looking ahead he saw a low church tower and walked on to that village. Some men were seated at a village inn, and they called to him, as he passed, to share in their refreshment. He took some bread and meat; and as he drank a draught of beer, heard those who were from London, talking about the murder. 'He has gone to Birmingham, they say,' said one: 'but they'll have him yet, for the scouts are out, and by to-morrow night there'll be a cry all through the country.'

He left off eating and hurried off, and walked till he almost dropped upon the ground; then he lay down in a lane, and had a long sleep in the middle of the day, yet it was always broken in upon by a reliving of the deed, til he knew not whether it was best to be asleep, or be awake, or to be dead. He wandered on, as irresolute and undecided as before, with the oppressive knowledge of another fearful solitary night coming onward toward him as the sun sank ever lower in the western sky.

Where was he headed? There was no place to go to. Suddenly, he took the desperate resolution of returning to London. 'There are people there, men and women, light, and bustle, that is what I need, there's somebody to speak to there, at all event,' he thought. 'there's always a hiding-place too. If they're after me in every other place they'll never expect me where I did it,. Why, I could lie by for a week or so, and, forcing blunt from Fagin, get to France. Damme, I'll risk it.'

He acted upon his latest impulse, with the firmest resolution, at last, and choosing the least frequented roads began, resolved to lie concealed within a short distance of the metropolis, to enter it at dusk by a circuitous route, to proceed straight to that part of it which he had fixed on for his destination.

The dog, though. If any description of him were out, it would not be forgotten that the dog had probably gone with him. This might lead to his apprehension. He resolved to drown him, and walked on, looking about for a pond: picking up a heavy stone and tying it to his handkerchief as he went. The animal looked up into his master's face while these preparations were made; whether his instinct apprehended something, or the robber's sidelong look at him was sterner than ordinary, he skulked farther to the rear than usual, and cowered as he came more slowly along. When his master halted at the brink of a pool, and looked round to call him, he stopped outright.

'Do you hear me call? Come here!' called Sikes.

The animal came up from the very force of habit; but as Sikes stooped, he uttered a low growl and started back.

'Come!' said the robber.

The dog wagged his tail, it advanced, retreated, paused and then ran at his hardest speed. The man whistled again and again, and sat down and waited. But no dog appeared, and he resumed his journey.

There is part of London, near to where the church at Rotherhithe abuts the Thames where the buildings on the banks are dirtiest and the vessels on the river blackest with the dust of colliers and the smoke of close-built low-roofed houses, there exists the filthiest, the strangest, the most extraordinary of the many localities of London, wholly unknown to the great mass of its inhabitants.

To reach it the visitor has to penetrate a maze of close, narrow, and muddy streets, and through the roughest and poorest of waterside people. The cheapest and least delicate provisions are heaped in the shops; the coarsest and commonest articles of apparel dangle at the salesman's door. Jostling with unemployed labourers, ballast-heavers, coal-whippers, brazen women, ragged children, and all the raff and refuse of the river, he might make his way, while assailed by offensive sights and smells from the narrow alleys which branch off, and deafened by the clash of ponderous waggons that bear piles of merchandise from the stacks of warehouses all around. Arriving in streets remoter and less-frequented, he would walk beneath tottering house-fronts that project over the pavement, dismantled walls that seem to totter as he passes, chimneys half hesitating to fall, windows guarded by rusty iron bars that time and dirt have almost eaten away, every imaginable sign of desolation and neglect.

In this neighbourhood, beyond Dockhead in the Borough of Southwark, is a muddy ditch, six or eight feet deep and fifteen or twenty wide when the tide is in, known as Folly Ditch. It is an inlet from the Thames, and can always be filled at high water by opening the sluices at the Lead Mills.

Here the buildings had crazy wooden galleries which were common to the backs of half a dozen of the houses, with holes; windows, broken and patched, with poles thrust out, on which to dry the linen that is never there; rooms so small, so filthy, so confined, that the air would seem too tainted even for the dirt and squalor which they shelter; wooden chambers thrusting themselves out above the mud, and threatening to fall into it - as some have done; there are dirt-besmeared walls and decaying foundations; every mark of poverty, every loathsome indication of filth, rot, and garbage; all these ornament the banks of Folly Ditch.

The warehouses are roofless and empty; the walls are crumbling; the windows are windows no more; the chimneys are blackened, but no longer yield smoke. Thirty or forty years ago, before losses and chancery suits came upon it, it was a thriving place; but now it is desolate. The houses have no owners; they are entered by those who have the courage; and there they live. They must have powerful motives for a secret residence, or be reduced to a destitute condition, those who seek refuge there.

In an upper room of one house - fair sized but ruinous in every other respect, and strongly defended at door and window - three men assembled, who sat in gloomy silence. Toby Crackit was one, another was Mr. Chitling, and the third a robber of fifty years age, whose nose had been almost beaten in, in old, or various, scuffles, and whose face bore a frightful scar. This man was a returned transport, and his name was Kags.

'When was Fagin took then?' Toby Crackit asked Chitling

'Two o'clock this afternoon..'

'And what of Bet?'

'Oh! Poor Bet! You couldn't believe it, if you hadn't seen it. She was beside herself, then she was required to see Nancy's body,' replied Chitling.

'Did she have to?' asked one of the others.

'Well, yes. To say who it was. Her and Nance were friends of old and always as thick as thieves; she went quite mad when she seen Nance, she was screaming and raving, I'm told, and beating her head against the walls. There were four men that had to hold her down; so they had to put a strait-weskut on her and took her to the hospital - and there she is. If she 'adn't who knows what she'd 'ave done, I think she could've done in Sikes for what he did. Th 'ospital is best place for her right now, for where else could she 'ave gone? there's nowhere else to go, all the people at the Cripples are in custody, I went up there and seen it with my own eyes.'

'The sessions are on,' said Kags: 'if they get the inquest over, and just one of them turns King's evidence: as, of course, one of them will - so that it isn't their neck that gets stretched - they can prove Fagin as an accessory before the fact; he'd be tried on Friday, and then he'd swing in six days, by God!'

'You should have heard the people,' said Chitling; 'And little wonder, given how popular Nancy was in the neighbourhood. The officers fought like devils, and they had to, they were forced to, or they'd have torn him away, and maybe torn him apart, I shouldn't wonder. He was down once and might've been trampled, 'e got a good kicking then, but the officers made a ring round him, and they fought their way along. You should have seen how he looked, all cut and bleeding and muddy, and he clung to the officers as if they were his dearest friends - he that always kept the greatest distance between himself and the like! I can see 'em, not able to stand upright with the pressing of the mob, and draggin' him along amongst 'em; I can see the people snarling to get at him; I can see the blood upon his hair and beard, and hear the cries with which the women worked themselves up...'

'Still. It wasn't Fagin who killed her, was it?' asked Kags.

'But 'e's implicated, isn't 'e? Anyway, those women swore they'd tear his heart out!'

'They'd have a long time looking for it!' Toby Crackit said. 'I don't think he ever had a heart!'

'Fagin's bad, yes. But like Kags says, has he ever killed anyone? - that you know of.' Chitling observed. 'And if that's what happened with 'im, what'll happen when Sikes is apprehended?'

'He'll get away,' Kags said. The other two men sat and looked at Kags, when a pat-pat-pattering noise was heard on the stairs, and Sikes's dog bounded into the room. The dog had jumped in at an open window downstairs, but, though they went out and looked for his master, he was not to be seen.

'He can't be coming here. I - I - hope not,' said Toby when they had returned.

'If he was coming he'd have come with the dog. Have you ever seen Bill Sikes without the dog?' said Kags stooping down to examine the animal, 'Here! Give us some water for him; he has run himself faint.'

Chitling watched the dog for some time as he drank. 'He's drunk it all up, every drop,' he said. 'He's lame, half-blind, he must have come a long way.'

'Which means *he's* a long way away. Where can he have come from!' exclaimed Toby. 'He's been to the other kens, and finding them filled with strangers come here, where he's been many a-time. But how comes he's here without the other!'

'He' - none of them called the murderer by his name - 'He can't have made away with himself. Do you think?' said Chitling.

Toby shook his head. 'He'd do it to someone else, but not to 'imself.'

THE FUGITIVE DIES BY HIS OWN ACTIONS WHILE SEEKING TO ESCAPE THE KING'S OFFICERS

It being dark now, the shutter was closed, and a candle lighted and placed upon the table. The terrible events of the last two days had made a deep impression on each, for it increased the danger and uncertainty of their own position. They drew their chairs closer They spoke little, and only in whispers, and were as silent and awe-stricken as if the remains of the murdered woman lay alongside them in the same room, for them to contemplate the many blunt wounds and hideous, livid bruising upon her murdered body.

Suddenly a hurried knocking was heard at the door below.

'It's young Bates,' said Kags, looking angrily round, to check the fear he felt himself.

The knocking came again. No. He never knocked like that.

One of them went to the window, and when he drew in his head back into the room he was shaking all over and his face was pale, while the dog was on the alert in an instant, and ran whining to the door. There was no need to tell the others who it was.

'We must let him in.'

'Isn't there any help for it?' asked the other in a hoarse voice.

'None.'

Crackit went down to the door, and returned followed by a man with the lower part of his face buried in a large handkerchief tied at the back of the neck, and another tied over his head under his hat. When he removed the handkerchiefs they saw he had a blanched face, sunken eyes, hollow cheeks, wasted flesh, a beard of three days' growth. He breathed short thick breaths. It was scarcely Bill Sikes at all, not as they had ever known him, it was as much the ghost of Sikes as anything they could imagine.

He laid his hand upon a chair in the middle of the room, he looked as though he was about to drop onto it; then, seeming to glance over his shoulder, he dragged it close to the wall - as close as it would go - and ground it against it - and sat down.

Not a word was exchanged. He looked at each in silence. If an eye were furtively raised and met his, it was instantly averted. When his hollow voice broke the silence all three started.

'How came that dog to be here?' he asked.

'Alone. Three hours ago.'

'To-night's paper says that Fagin's took. Is it true?' Sikes asked.

'True.' A single word was all that was required to convey the import. Just one word conveyed the ending of a lifetime of graft; so they were silent again.

'Damn you all!' said Sikes, passing his hand across his forehead. 'Have you nothing to say to me?'

'Damn you for what you've done to us all!' Kags said. Sikes looked malevolently at him.

'Bet's gone mad,' Chitling said as casually as he could, struggling to keep an accusatory tone from his voice, which was far from being an effortless endeavour; and that was all that any of them said of the murder.

'You that keep this house,' said Sikes, turning his face to Crackit, 'do you mean to sell me, or let me lie here till the hunt is over and I can get away to some other place?'

'You may stop here, if you think it safe,' replied Crackit, with some reluctance.

Sikes narrowed his eyes, 'If I think it is safe?' he repeated. 'Well is it, or isn't it safe?' he demanded. But his attention slid away from his own question in the following instant, his eyes moved slowly up the wall behind him: rather *trying* to turn his head than actually doing it: then he looked up the wall to the ceiling on the opposite side of the room; just as he had done in *that other room*, following the spatter of blood with his eye,

Asudden knock. Crackit left the room and came back with Charley Bates. Sikes sat opposite the door, so that the moment the boy entered the room he encountered his figure.

'Toby,' said the boy falling back, as Sikes turned his eyes towards him, 'why did you not tell me of this, downstairs?'

Sikes started to interrogate the others.

'Is it - the body, I mean - is it buried?'

They shook their heads, all except Charley Bates; *'The body?'*he exclaimed. 'You mean Nance? Nancy. Who *you* murdered?' he accused, rather than said.

Sikes ignored Charley Bates reply. 'Why isn't it!' he retorted with a glance at the wall behind him. 'Wot do they keep such things above the ground for?'

'The inquest,' Kags said shortly.

'I can't stay in this room,' said Charley Bates, 'Not with '*im*. Let me go into another room,'

Charley!' said Sikes, stepping forward. 'Don't you - don't you know me?'

'I knw you! and you'd better not come near me,' answered the boy looking, with horror in his eyes, upon the murderer's face. 'You are the monster! Don't you know wot you did? Nance was like a mother to us! The closest thing to a mother that any of us ever knowed! It was either her, or Fagin, an' who'd want to admit to 'aving Nat Fagin as either mother or father!'

Sikes, prompted by the accusatory tone, launched himself at the young pick-pocket but he stopped half-way across the room. They looked at each other; but Sikes's eyes sunk gradually to the ground.

'Witness you three,' cried the boy, shaking, and becoming more and more excited as he spoke. 'Witness - I'm not afraid of 'im - if they come here after him, I'll give him up. He'll have no safe place, wherever I am! I'll show them up here! Let me into another room, or I'll have him! I tell you that. He may kill me for it if he likes, but if I'm here I'll give him up. If there's any pluck in any of you three, you'll help me.' He paused. Then added a single word, which he flung with accusatory vehemence at Sikes; 'Murderer!'

Sikes flared up again and appeared as though he would launch himself from his seat at the boy, indeed he arose from his seat but instead he turned around and skulked back to sit upon the chair again. He looked, with horror, behind himself at the blank wall, and at the quivering shadows as they were cast upon the wall by the figures in the room in the low candlelight. As Sikes had his entire senses filled with the image of Nancy appearing from out of these shadows to confront him, he was unready when, pouring out cries, and accompanying them with violent gestures, the boy threw himself, single-handed, upon the strong man. In it's suddenness and the intensity of energy he knocked Sikes from the chair and onto the roughly hewn floor.

The three others seemed stupefied and offered neither aid nor hinderence to either. The boy and man rolled on the ground together; the boy remained entirely heedless of the blows that were being showered upon him. The contest was too unequal to last. Sikes had him down and had his knee on his throat, til the boy looked to be have become quite senseless. But Sikes could not hold the middle of the room; with the small heaped figure beneath him, he remembered that he must be against the wall, he must have his back to the wall, lest Nancy reappeared behind him.

As Crackit stooped to pull Sikes off the boy, Sikes had, with a look of alarm, incomprehensible to the others, freely got off him and leapt at the chair and jammed his back to the wall, with the sound of a growl and whimper in his throat, and he kept his look over his shoulder, always upon the wall.

Crackit pointed to the window. While three panes were boarded with cardboard it was through the single pane of glass that they saw lights gleaming from the board-walk alley below and voices were heard in loud and earnest conversation, followed by the tramp of hurried footsteps crossing the nearest wooden bridge - there were many footsteps, so many that they seemed endless in number. There must have been at least one man on horseback among the crowd below; for there was the noise of hoofs rattling on the uneven boards. The gleam of lights increased and shone through the single pane of glass and played about the ceiling; the footsteps came more noisily on. Then, came a loud knocking at the door, and a hoarse murmur from such a multitude of angry voices as would have made the boldest quail.

With Sikes' knee removed from his throat, the boy seemed to revive; hearing the commotion below he sprang back to new life.

'Help!' he shrieked in a voice that rent the air. 'Murderer! Here!'

Many voices sounded from below;

- 'Murder!'

- 'He's here!'

- 'In the King's name, open the door.'

- 'Break in the door!'

'Break down the door! Break it down!' screamed the boy. 'There are scoundrels and accomplices here! I tell you they'll never open it to you. Break in the door and run to the room where the light is. Break it!'

A loud huzzah burst from the crowd as hard strokes, thick and heavy, slammed against the door.

Sikes leapt from his chair. 'Open the door of another room where I can lock away this screeching Hell-babe,' he cried fiercely; he grabbed the boy and dragged him as easily as if he were an empty sack.

'That door. Quick!'

He flung him into the other room, bolted it, and turned the key. 'Is the downstairs door locked?'

'Double-locked and chained,' replied Crackit.

'The panels - they are strong?'

'Lined with sheet-iron.'

'Good. And the windows too?'

'Yes, and the windows.'

The desperate fugitive, threw the sash up and yelled out at the menacing crowd, 'Damn you! Damn you all! She was a snitch! Do your worst! I'll cheat you yet!'

Of all the terrific yells that ever fell on mortal ears, none could exceed the cry of the infuriated throng. Some shouted to those who were nearest to set the house on fire; others roared to the officers to shoot him dead. The man on horseback threw himself out of the saddle, and burst through the crowd as if he were parting water, and cried up to that window, in a voice that, despite the roaring fury, rose above all others, 'Twenty guineas, to be paid immediately, to the man who brings him down!' And he waved a small suede pouch above his head. The nearest voices took up the cry, and hundreds more echoed it to the few, furthest away, who may not have heard it. Some called for ladders, some for sledge-hammers; some ran with torches to-and-fro as if to seek them, some pressed forward in a madman's ecstasy, and thus impeded the progress of all the others as they endeavoured some wild action of their own; the crowd seemed to be acting without reason or direction in this common purpose; indeed, that was precisely the outcome of all their activity. For all their noise and energy, there was only one common success, from time to time, they would all join in one loud furious roar.

'The tide,' the murderer said to the three men, 'the tide was in as I came up. Give me a rope, a long rope. While they're all in front I may drop into Folly's Ditch and clear off. Give me a rope, or I shall do three more murders.'

'Why did you let 'im in? For us to be murdered?' murmured one of the three as each of the panic-stricken men pointed to where there was rope lying in coils. The murderer, selected the longest and strongest, and hurried to the top of the house. When he emerged on the roof by a door there, a loud shout proclaimed it to those who remained at the front, they immediately began to pour round, pressing upon each other in an unbroken stream.

Sikes fixed a board, which he had carried up for the purpose, so firmly against the door that it would be a great difficulty to open it from the inside; he crept over the tiles, and looked over the low parapet. The water was out, and the ditch was a bed of mud.

The crowd was hushed as it watched him and doubtful of his purpose, but the instant they perceived it, his intent was defeated. They all raised a cry of triumph to which all their previous shouting had only been whispers. Again and again it rose.

The people pressed on - on, on, in a strong struggling current of angry faces. The houses on the opposite side of the ditch had been entered by the mob; the sash windows were thrown up, or even torn out of their rotting brickwork housings; there were tiers and tiers of faces in every window; cluster upon cluster of people.

'They have him now,' cried a man.

'Hurrah! Hurrah!' shouted the crowd over and over.

'I will give fifty pounds,' cried another old gentleman, 'to the man who takes him alive. I will remain here, till he comes to ask me for it.'

Another roar went up on hearing this, and the crowd pushed forward again. There was another roar as the word was passed among the crowd that the internal door had been forced, and that the room had been entered. The stream abruptly turned, and the people at the windows, seeing those upon the bridges pouring back, quit their places and, running into the street, joined the concourse that now thronged pell-mell to the spot they had all left: all panting to get near, to look upon the criminal as the officers brought him out.

There were cries and shrieks from those who were pressed almost to suffocation, or trampled underfoot in the confusion; the narrow ways were completely blocked between the rush of some to regain the space in front of the house, and the struggles of others to get away from the mass, so that the immediate attention of the mob was distracted from the murderer.

Sikes had shrunk, being quelled both by the ferocity of the crowd and by being struck by the impossibility of his escape. Seeing that they were distracted, he sprang to his feet, determined to make a last effort for his life by dropping into the ditch, and to creep away in the darkness and confusion. Roused to new strength and energy by the noise within the house which announced to him that the crowd had entered, he set his foot against the stack of chimneys; he fastened one end of the rope tightly and firmly round it, and with the other made a strong running noose by the aid of his hands and teeth, all done in a moment. The rope was long enough to let himself down by the cord almost to the ground, he took out his blade from his pocket ready to cut the rope and let him drop the rest of the way and then to make his getaway.

He brought the loop over his head to slip it beneath his arm-pits, when the old gentleman (who clung so tight to the railing of the bridge as to resist the force of the crowd) called out to those about him that the attempted fugitive was about to lower himself. The murderer on the roof was suddenly insensible to all that went on below, for, as he turned and looked behind he saw *the eyes,* and the bloodied head; he was lost, he knew; she was to be revenged upon him. He uttered a yell of unearthly terror.

'The eyes! It's the eyes again!' he cried out in a groan. He staggered as if he had been struck by a sudden blow by a champion ring-fighter, he lost his balance and tumbled over the edge of the roof. The noose ran up with his weight falling against it, til it was around his neck and it closed and tightened as swiftly as an arrow's flight. He fell for a full thirty-five feet when there was a tremendous jerk as the rope reached it's limit, and the body was flung out at the end of the rope with a terrific convulsion of the limbs into a circling pendulum motion; and there he hung. The open knife, held ready in his hand, was knocked out of his dying grip and dropped into Folly's Ditch. The old chimney quivered with the shock, but stood. In the filth and squalor of the squalid neighbourhood the metal blade shone brightly, by the light of the many burning torches that were carried by the crowd, upon the turgid mud of the river inlet.

The murderer, having fallen so close to the ground, continued to swing, broken and lifeless, in decreasing circles, with the feet of the dead man only slightly above the reach of the upstretched arms of the mob. The attending officers entered the building to cut the body down from the chimney stack. As they worked at cutting the rope to let the body drop to the ground, a white dog appeared and ran backwards and forwards on the parapet with a dismal howl. It readied itself at the edge of the roof to spring at the dead man's shoulders. It leapt, but missed his aim, and fell into Folly's Ditch striking his head against a stone and dashed out his brains.

Having accomplished the task of taking down the body the officers then moved to release the boy, Charley Bates, whose attack upon the murderer and whose cries had carried on down from the room to a passing officer below, and he was released from his temporary prison.

FAGIN IS CONDEMNED AND SENT TO THE GALLOWS; HIS LAST NIGHT ALIVE

The court was filled, from floor to roof, with faces. Eager and inquisitive, the eyes peered and all their looks were fixed upon one man - Fagin. Before him and behind: above, below, on the right and on the left: he seemed to stand surrounded by a firmament of gleaming eyes. He had been wounded with some missiles from the crowd on the day of his capture, and his head was bandaged with a linen cloth.

For all his lifetimes work, of grabbing and grasping and grafting, and coining, and thieving, and dealing in stolen goods, and so many other ways of making a living, he stood in the grand court in all his drab and tattered attire, with one hand that rested before him, and the other held to his ear, and his head thrust forward so he could catch every word from the presiding judge. At times, he turned his eyes to the jurymen to observe the effect of the slightest feather-weight in his favour; and when a point was made against him with terrible distinctness, he looked towards his counsel, in mute appeal that he would urge some matter in his behalf.

It was his *eyes* that spoke for him, as they moved about, looking this way and then that, barely moving the head itself and otherwise not stirring a hand nor foot. He had scarcely moved since the trial began; and now although the judge had ceased to speak, he remained in the same strained attitude of close attention.

Aslight bustle in the court recalled him to himself. Without moving his head, but his eyes only, he saw that all the jurymen had turned together to consider their verdict. He let his eyes wander to the gallery; he could see the people rising above each other in densely crowded tiers, to see *him*: A few seemed unmindful of him, and looked only to the jury in impatient wonder of how they could delay in considering the verdict of "guilty". But in not one face - not even among the women, of whom there were many - could he read the faintest sympathy with himself, could only read an all-absorbing interest that he should be condemned.

As he saw this all in one bewildered glance, a death-like stillness came upon the courtroom again and, looking back, he saw that the jurymen had turned towards the judge.

Hush!

The courtroom awaited the verdict of the jury, though all there, bar the jurymen, seemed to have determined he was guilty. But it was not the verdict, they only sought permission to retire. If there was more to discuss, Fagin thought, and not the instant condemnation he fancied the gallery wished to see, perhaps there was a place for hope.

He looked, wistfully, into the jurymen's faces, one by one when they passed out, as though to see which way the greater number leant; but it was fruitless. The jailer touched him on the shoulder. The man pointed out a chair in the corner of the box, or else he would not have seen it, and he sat down .

He looked up into the gallery again. Some of the people were eating, and some fanning themselves with handkerchiefs; for the crowded place had become very hot. There was one young man sketching his face in a note-book; he wondered whether he was achieving a good likeness. In the same way, when he turned his eyes towards the judge, his mind began to busy itself with the fashion of his dress, and what it cost; although never affording such garb himself, he nonetheless knew the price of each item that was about the judge's person.

As he looked idly about the courtroom his mind was not, for an instant, free from one oppressive overwhelming sense of the grave that opened at his feet; it was ever present, yet it was so only in a vague and general way, and he could not fix his thoughts upon it. A guilty verdict would open that grave up to him and hurl him into it within a few days, yet still it seemed at a great distance. Even while he trembled at the idea of speedy execution, he fell to counting the iron spikes before him, and wondering how the head of one had been broken off, and whether they would mend it, or leave it. Then he thought of the scaffold - he had seen many swing from it in his youngest days, for the entertainment , but as his career had progressed he had long since sworn off being a spectator; while at the thought of how he was to be put upon that platform his mind baulked - so he watched a man sprinkling the floor to cool it.

At some length there was a cry for silence, and a breathless look from all towards the door as the jury returned. He could glean nothing from their faces.

Perfect stillness ensued - not a rustle - not a breath.

The verdict came.

Guilty.

The court room rang out with a tremendous shout, and another carried on through the building, and another, it seemed, came from the street outside, and then it echoed and gathered strength as the shouts swelled. It became a peal of joy from the populace, as though for the announcement of a holiday, a festival or a feast, all greeting the news that he would die on Monday, for the sentence must be death by hanging.

The noise subsided, and he was asked if he had anything to say why sentence of death should not be passed. He looked intently at his questioner; but it was necessary to repeat it twice before he seemed to hear it; he only muttered that he was an old man - an old man, he repeated - dropping to a whisper he added, (though his death still seemed at a very great distant from him), and surely old age would as soon carry him off as execution, and why trouble a hangman for his neck and his slight weight, as though he were a feather that drift in the air from the end of the rope. He was silent again.

The judge assumed the fearful black cap. A woman in the gallery, uttered some exclamation; the prisoner looked up; and the judge looked too, as if he were angry at the interruption. The address was solemn; the sentence fearful and inevitable. Fagin stood without motion, his eyes darted about in his haggard face, but, otherwise, his face betrayed no comprehension of the import of the pronouncement of the sentence. Then the jailer put his hand upon his arm, and beckoned him. He gazed stupidly about him for an instant, and obeyed.

They led him through a paved room under the court, where some prisoners were waiting till their turn came, and others were talking to friends, who crowded round a grate which looked into the open yard. The prisoners fell back to make him visible to the visitors who were clinging to the bars: they all assailed him with names, screeched and hissed. He shook his fist, and would have spat upon them; but the jailers hurried him on through a gloomy passage lighted only by a few dim lamps, into the interior of the prison.

He was searched, that he might not have about him the means of anticipating the judgement of the law; then they led him to one of the condemned cells, and left him - alone. If he could have had a visitor it would have been from his own trained thieves, but they had all either been arrested, or those that had not were necessarily unable to attend; and Nancy Porter and Bill Sikes could not visit; he had warned Bill not to be hasty, it was Sikes that had brought him to this cell. But Sikes had escaped the inevitable judgement through his own desperate misadventure, and had abandoned his old tutor, employer, and associate to take the brunt of the state's judgement, to face the court, and the anger of the populace.

He sat on a stone bench opposite the door, which served for seat and bedstead; and casting his blood-shot eyes upon the ground, tried to collect his thoughts. After a while, he began to remember a few disjointed fragments of what the judge had said: though it had seemed to him that he could not hear a word. These fell into place, and by degrees suggested more: so that in a little time he had the whole of it. He was to be hanged by the neck, till he was dead. That was it. To be hanged by the neck till he was - dead. How that crowd had roared with relief and joy to hear it.

The cell had been built for many years. Scores of men must have passed their last hours there. As it became dark, he began to think of all the men he had known who had died upon the scaffold; some had died through his intercession. The faces that he knew rose up, in quick succession, so that he could hardly count them all. Some of them might have inhabited that cell; sat *there*! He had seen some of them die - and had joked too, because they had died with prayers upon their lips. With what a rattling noise the drop went down; and how suddenly they changed. Often they were strong and vigorous men, and became dangling heaps, seemingly of little more substance than their reeking clothes in that moment.

As he sat and reflected inwardly on this, it had, being mid-autumn, become darker; and now it was dark, very dark. Dark. He felt the dark, and it felt like an overcoat over him, but this coat gave no warmth or comfort; why didn't they bring a light?

Light, light! He must have light; he would weep if he could not have light - and Fagin never wept, had not wept since, he was maybe five, or six, or seven years old. He must have light! Light, to release him from the oppression of this deathly dark. At length, when his hands were raw with beating against the heavy door, two men appeared: one bearing a candle, which he thrust into an iron candlestick fixed against the wall: the other dragging in a mattress on which to pass the night; for the prisoner was to be left alone no more.

Then came the night - dark, dismal, silent night. Others are glad to hear the church-clock strike, for they tell of the coming of day and new life. To him they brought deepening despair. The boom of every bell came laden with the one, deep, hollow sound - the slow, steady, ever oncoming, booming footsteps of Death. What were the noise and bustle of cheerful morning, which penetrated even here, to him? Such sounds added mockery to his position.

The day passed off.

Day? There was no day; it was gone as soon as it had come, it was a mere brief interval before the onset of night again; night so long, long in its dreadful silence; and yet so short, short in its fleeting hours that were like a vapour. At one time he raved and blasphemed; at another he howled and tore his hair. Venerable men of his own persuasion had come to pray by him, but he had driven them away. They renewed their charitable efforts, but he would not have it, it was too late for seeking comfort in ancient promises.

Saturday night already. So soon. He had only one night more. As he reflected on this, so fleeting did his thoughts seem, that he was astonished when day broke - Sunday.

For all his dread it was not until the night of this last awful day that a withering sense of his helpless state came in its full intensity upon his blighted soul; not that he had ever held any defined or positive hope of mercy; he had never been able to consider more than the dim probability of dying.

He had spoken little to either of the two men, who relieved each other in their attendance upon him; and they, for their parts, made no effort to talk to him. It was their grim duty only.

The condemned criminal sat on his stone bed, rocking himself from side to side, with the face more of a snared beast than that of any man. His mind was evidently wandering to his old life, for he continued to mutter, without appearing conscious to anything other than to the internal image, as part of his vision of continuing life. As the hours of the day passed to night - his last night - and his remaining life continued to rapidly diminish, he cowered rather than sat or lay upon the stone bed; he did not sleep but remained awake while drifting into dreaming, and thought of the past.

'Jeb knows the ropes. An' now he's going to hang from one, ha!' - 'How is an honest thief to make a living if they keep hanging my best workers.' - 'Tell me your name? Bill Sikes, you say? And how old are you? Eight, my dear. Well, you'll not see your ninth year if you can't thieve better than that. I'll show you how to do it properly...' - 'Tell me, Mr Catchpole, d'yer have a sister?' - 'Good work, Charley - well done....' - 'There you are, Nancy. You're sure to snare a good man, with looks like yours...' - 'Try again, Dodger, try again.' - 'Oliver, too, ha! Oliver too... oh, look at him, he's quite the gentleman now!' - 'It's rather more than it ought to be, my dear; but as I know you'll do me a good turn another time...' - 'Bolter's throat, Bill; never mind the girl. Bolter's throat as deep as you can cut.' - ' Saw his head off!' - 'An old man, my Lord; I am but a very, very old man!' - 'Tell them I've gone to sleep, they'll believe you. You can get me out.' - 'Now then, now then, now then!'

His eyes shone with a terrible light; his flesh, unwashed, crackled with the fever that burnt him. Seven o'clock - Eight o'clock - Nine. If it was not a trick to frighten him, then those were the real hours treading on each other's heels. It seemed that yet another struck before the voice of the previous hour had ceased to vibrate throughout the cast iron of the bell!

He started up, and with a gasping, dry mouth, he hurried to-and-fro around the small cell. He had feared the dark on the first night; now the cell itself was too small; too, too small; it could not contain his energy; he must walk. He was in a paroxysm of fear and wrath that even the jailer - used to such sights - recoiled from what he saw. Fagin grew so terrible in all the tortures of his evil conscience, that the one jailer could not bear to sit with him alone, and had to fetch his duty companion, and so the two kept watch together.

The dreadful walls of Newgate, which have hidden so much misery and unspeakable anguish, not only from the eyes, but, too often and too long, from the thoughts of men, those walls had never beheld so dread a spectacle. The few who ever wondered what the man, who was to be hanged on-the-morrow, was doing on their last night, would have slept ill if they could have seen him there.

From early in the evening until nearly midnight, little groups of two and three persons presented themselves at the lodge-gate, and inquired anxiously whether any reprieve had been received. By degrees these people fell away, one by one; and, for an hour or two, in the dead of night, the street outside the prison was left to solitude and darkness. None had arrived to enquire about Fagin, none had interceded on behalf of Fagin. There was no one to intercede for him. There was to be no reprieve.

Fagin had sat down, he was nervously exhausted as much as physically fatigued from both his raving and all his circled wanderings in that cell throughout the previous day. He slept. It was the only night of refreshing sleep he had there during his short tenure.

The morning hours passed. Two o'clock. Three o'clock. Four o'clock. Five o'clock. Six o'clock. There was a grating through which, as day dawned, came the sound of men's voices, mingled with the noise of hammering, and the throwing down of boards. They were putting up the scaffold. He could not hear them, Fagin slept.

The church-clock chimed his final hour. The door of the cell opened, and the escorts walked in. Nat Fagin still slept. The men laid firm hands upon him and shook him awake. He woke drowsily at their rude shaking and he seemed to wonder where he was and why he had been awakened from such refreshing comforting sleep; then his mind seemed to leap to full realisation. He struggled with the power of desperation against the hold they had on him, but only for an instant; then he sent up cry upon cry that echoed in the small cell and carried throughout the cell block, that penetrated even each of those massive walls until they reached the open yard. He was so weak that he hardly had the strength to walk. From this place, he was partly led and partly carried, or dragged; they passed through several strong gates, opened by turnkeys from the inner side.

Day had dawned when they emerged into the yard outside the prison, yet it remained in chill shadow, the sun having not yet risen to such a height as to light or heat it. Fagin shivered, yet it was hardly the cold of the air that caused it. A multitude had assembled; the windows were filled with people, some smoking, some eating, others playing cards, someone in the crowd was playing popular tunes on a trumpet; the crowd were talking, hailing friends, quarrelling, joking, pushing. Among all who were gathered there some were the family, or associates, of those that were to be hung; they did not join in; they stood silently, dreading what was to come. But they were few in so large a crowd. Yet more people arrived and gathered around the fringes, or took up some point as they considered to offer the best view of the spectacle. Everybody in that open yard told of life, of animation, but not for Fagin.

It is true that everybody there did, indeed, tell of life and animation; except for the purpose that they were all gathered; but not every *thing* spoke of the same life and animation. That purpose was told in the cluster of objects in the centre of the yard. They told it all - the platform made of thick planks, the five steps up to the platform, the cross-beam, the noosed rope, the hangman in his mask, the stack of roughly made coffins behind the platform. The apparatus and props on that black and drear stage upon which is played out all the hideous spectacle and gross drama of lawful execution.

Fagin quailed, and sought, with his little remaining strength, to back away. The escorts held firmly onto his arms and guided him, using their overwhelming strength; two sturdy men against an old withered man, up the steps onto the platform and toward the hangman. Before the noose was placed over his head he could sense the grizzled horsehair against his neck...

AFTERWORD

The news of the murder had spread abroad by a variety of means, the household staff at the homes of Mr Brownlow and Miss Rose Maylie knew of it by word-of-mouth; it was included in bulletins, it appeared in the London newspapers too; when it was first published, the news was only that there had been a murder in Spitalfields; it did not cause Rose Maylie any cause to wonder. Then it had emerged that it was a young woman that had been killed, this piqued a shiver of concern that bordered on fear but the limited information given in the reports was inconclusive. A few days later, a full account of the events, as far as such events are ever fully known when both the victim and the perpetrator are no longer alive to give their account; the newspaper gave the name of the murderer, who had died by misadventure while being pursued by the King's officers and an accompanying mob, and also the name of the victim. It confirmed that first tremble of misgiving that Rose Maylie had experienced. With the receipt of this news her tender heart was sorely injured; she was quite inconsolable and wept for many days.

Among those published details that she could bear to read, and those that others read to her when the tears so obscured her sight that she could no longer read, the one that excited the greatest quantity of her prodigious and piteous tears was that of the mystery, such as it was, of a well-made pair of cream kid-gloves, embroidered with the letters R.M., that had been found clutched fast in the dead girl's hands. It was supposed that they had not belonged to the victim originally, since they were of such good quality and would have cost several months rent for her to have bought them. It was assumed they had come to her through her criminal friends; this last detail was not included in the newspaper reports, but it was included as a supposition in the report of the investigation into the crime. To young Rose Maylie how those gloves had come into the other woman's possession was not a mystery.

Rose reflected how that other young woman, Nancy Porter, wretch that she was, had put herself into the gravest danger, in full knowledge of the hazard, comprehending it and yet accepting it. When anyone is seen in youthful vigour, it seems beyond all expectations to hear of their death, in this instance, within days, even allowing for the young girls prediction of her own end. The girl knew it; she had stated it, and had predicted it would be soon. But, it had come so soon; could she have known this too? She had said that Old Father Thames would enclose itself over her head. She had said that the river was a friend to those with no one to care for, and no one to mourn them, so they go to the river and have it embrace them when they go from this life.

It was not to be; her end had been of the most brutish kind. This could be divined from those newspaper reports that had excised the worst of it, but it could be imagined. The imagining of it would cause greater distress to Rose Maylie; and raised her to an ever greater anguish. It prompted a question, that could never be satisfactorily answered, to leap to her mind; how had this tyrant, who ruled over her, could possibly have known of their meeting; or had her murder been because of the usual way he treated her; for she had shown some of the marks upon her body; had shown the marks of this other variety of - love? - it was a form of love that baffled the comprehension of Miss Maylie; it was true, that the girl had never used the word, yet Rose sensed this was the nature of the binding between her and the man who had murdered her; mysterious as it was to her; moreso since she also sensed the girl, paradoxically, loathed her condition, but had become dependent upon it as certainly as if she had been chained to her fate, Cassandra-like.

And she had said that her death would never reach me, Rose reflected ruefully. No matter how debased the person, the act of murder is not only the greater crime, over their own crimes no matter how prolific, (short of a murder committed by themselves); any murder is taken to be a crime against the entire society and not against the single victim alone, for even the highest and most exalted citizen has no greater right to their own bare life than the most debased or depraved.

All this, all these tears, were a great puzzle to Oliver Twist, who that delightful young lady held tightly to her at such moments; he attempted to understand the depth of the passion his protector had fallen into; and he sought for words of comfort to release her from her anguish, but, much as he did try, his young mind could not comprehend it.

In time, the young lady reflected; Oliver must know. He gives thanks in his prayers to myself, to my aunt Mrs Maylie, to Mr Brownlow, to the nurse Miss Bedwin, to his own, unknown to him, mother; he gives his thanks to so many, but not to her, not to Nancy Porter. For all the aid we sought to offer, and have brought to him, none of us will be asked, or expected, or required, to offer our lives for his sake; to suffer such a sanction as she had. She had full knowledge of the possible consequence, knew that it *may* happen, yet she had offered her help regardless. Oliver must know of this, and must know of her, Rose was certain; but not of her fate, at least, not now. He must know that too, in time, but not now.

THE FINAL WORD

Nearly a full decade has passed, Rose Maylie, married and the happy mother of a happy brood, and still in all the bloom and grace of her young womanhood, makes her way, during summer, through sultry fields during the middle afternoon until she comes to the lively city, simmering in the heat of that season. She follows a familiar course, to the graveyard of the grand classical styled Church of the Holy Trinity, built a hundred years before, in the borough of Spitalfields, when the borough still had the character of a village with paths that wandered out into open country. This walk - for she always walks, never does she take a carriage or a cab regardless of the weather - takes the form of a pilgrimage. She arrives at that church as the shadows are lengthening in the late afternoon. Midway along the left-side of the church-yard, unkempt in high summer, for the grass is allowed to grow naturally, there is a very small headstone in the cooling shade by the wall; it stands little higher than a kerbstone, and can be hard to locate; upon it is carved the words common to many gravestones, 'Sacred to the memory of...' then below is the name, 'Nancy Ellen Porter'. Having attended to the very small space that her grave occupies, and having cleared the old and withered blooms and laid down fresh flowers, the young lady goes into the church to offer a prayer.

When she first made the journey she had tried to remember the form of words that she had cried out to the girl when they had parted on that night by the foggy river; she had not intended such words as a prayer; yet they would serve as such. She attempted to recollect those words exactly as she had called them out; for they had been entirely extemporised, unthought of the moment before she had said them, yet they were apposite at the moment, and had proved prescient and appropriate, for the bleakest of reasons. From those words, so far as she could recollect them - her sudden and immediate thoughts in the moment - she formed the prayer that she always offered for Nancy: 'May God reserve some special place for those that overcome their mean circumstances and their hopelessness to help...' What else had she said on that occasion? 'To help...? A child who might have otherwise been forced to follow your path?' She had known that she had added a comment about her kindness, and how she had overcome all the circumstances that had made her, by her act of needful aid. Could she sincerely add, 'suffer not the little children?' for while it applied to Oliver, the girl herself had suffered dreadfully, as no one should, from her youngest years. She struggled to recollect her own words, and had suceeded in it, and had jotted them on the inner cover of her small bible. This was the prayer she always said for the memory of Nancy Porter. It had taken on the character of a personal tradition in her own mind.

And yet, Rose knew, her suffering was so commonplace too. This further reflection would cause the young lady to be overwhelmed again by the vast dimensionlessness of all the suffering; of that she had witnessed, and also of that which was hidden, yet which see sensed, not only in the life of Nancy Porter, but in all the streets, lanes and alleyways of that city, and far beyond. Although the girl had been subjected to the worst of sufferings, and had been brought to her death by further blunt brutality, she had done so for the noblest reasons; all this from a place, in this person, where no nobility might be suspected to have resided. So she added to her prayer, in conclusion, 'suffer not the children', for that young woman, Nancy, would not allow the child, Oliver Twist, to suffer as she had been forced to by her neglected circumstances.

Rose Maylie, despite her own personal happiness in all other parts of her life, would think of the girl, still, with deep sadness and regret, and could not help but be puzzled at her clinging to he that had killed her; after a period of years she would still think of her, although no longer with convulsive sobs, but with some softly spilling tears only. Some times she would think of her, even wondered what life would have been like for her if she had lived, if she could have lived long, for the girl herself had predicted she would never live a long life.

Rose Maylie would sometimes think of the girl's name, and repeat it over in her mind; then she would hear the name being spoken, just as she heard it called out to her by the river in answer to her query, as clearly as though the young woman were there in the flesh, close by but partly obscured by the dense river fog, and calling it out to her again in a loud whisper, 'Nancy. My name is Nancy... Nancy Porter.'

The Gutter Press has several imprints, among them are; Ventures in Recycled Fiction, FictionFaction, A. Bridge & Co., Essential Editions and Oxbury Universal Press. Here is a selection of some of the titles that are currently available, and others that are to become available soon.

Although these titles may be stocked anywhere, it is best to check the Amazon, Kindle and Kobo websites, and websites of other E-readers and formats.

ETERNAL BELOVED by BELLE ELLIS (New Ventures in Recycled Fiction/FictionFaction) is, both an abridgement and an extension of Emily Bronte's Wuthering Heights, which maintains the original plot, excises or summarizes some episodes but also expands upon some of the mystical elements of the original novel.

> *'Earth is so fair, yet I think Heaven will be glorious too.*
> *I hope it will be much as this place is, or I'll have no use for it.'*

I knocked my knuckles through the glass, and stretched out my arm to seize the branch. Yet, instead of grasping a dry branch, my hand closed around the fingers of a little, moist, ice-cold hand! The intense horror of my nightmare struck me: I tried to draw back my arm, but I now found that I no longer had a grip on the hand, but it was my hand that was in the grip of this, other, icy hand, and it clung to me; and it would not release me.

A most melancholy voice sobbed, 'Let me in - let me in!'- 'Who are you?' I cried out, while I struggled to disengage myself. 'Catherine,' it replied shiveringly, 'I'm come home. I lost my way while walking on the moor! It seems so long since I was here.' As it spoke, I could discern, obscurely, a child's face resolve itself from the snowy gloom. It was the face, as surely as the recollection of a dream will allow, of the young but surly, 'good-fairy' I had met earlier. If not, it was her double, her twin, her sister, her doppelganger, or her daughter, or so I thought (why did I think it was her *daughter*?). The girl sobbed, she begged, she wheedled, she pleaded; all the while her hair was cast about her face in the wuthering snowstorm, there were snowflakes caught in her hair. All the time she clung to my arm regardless of how I tried to shake her loose; she was but a girl, yet her grasp was super-natural. Terror made me cruel; and, finding it useless to attempt shaking her - or, whatever this vision may be - off, I pulled the arm toward me through the smashed pane. Horror piled upon horror at the sight, in the candle-light within the closeted casement, of her ghoulishly blue-white hand and fore-arm, it seemed the arm of someone between life and death, of a person beset by tuberculosis, still well rounded but displaying the signs of wasting and withering. Cruelly, I rubbed the arm to-and-fro across the broken glass, till real blood ran from the arm of this ghostly vision and soaked the bedclothes: yet, still it wailed on, quite heedless of my action. 'Let me in!' she repeated, while it maintained its tenacious hold. I could not - *could not* - release that grip. I sensed that I could have drained the entire person, drained her slight frame of all her blood, yet still it would maintain its hold! How could it be? Yet it was! ....

... Her attention was roused. 'Nelly!' she exclaimed, 'I thought I was gone from this world. That all in this room, and out there,' she nodded toward the open window, 'were only colourful shadows, that distracted me, I was not certain were I was. But I am still here! How much longer though?' She paused, and when she began again, she started on another thought. 'When I was young...'

'You *are* young, ma'am. You have many more days ahead of you. Far more than those behind you,' I said, although I knew it could not be true.

'Ah, Nelly! you know that cannot be so. When I was a girl, I would become gloomy sometimes....'

'And now you're being gloomy again.' I interrupted. 'Think of life, ma'am. To live, you must *want* to live.'

'...there were times I didn't take joy in anything. However, when I emerged from it, each time, it was as though I had been renewed; I then took greater joy in all those small things I enthused to you about, remember? It must have seemed odd to you, I never let on to the cause, but that is what it was.

'Then, afterwards, when I watched a linnet build its nest, take a mate, and watch the eggs hatch, and the birds grow to maturity in turn; there was life, always renewing, in that sight and so many others like it, in that I derived joy.

'Now my fleet days are closing, as surely as the sun setting on a summers day. I have survived, but how am I to live? To merely endure? Fever, or pain, and endurance, is all you offer me. No! I know my day is darkening...; to lose Self, to cease, to be beyond thought and worldly bounds; to seek the other land beyond the oceans of Life, the shores of Oblivion...'

=

INNOCENCE / GUILT by ANTOSHA CHECKHONTE (New Ventures in Recycled Fiction/FictionFaction), with extensive additional material by Grigori Shologanov, is a novella of love, deception, jealousy and murder set in, and originally published, in Russia, at the end of the nineteenth century. After the murder, the story becomes one of investigation and detection.

An affable stranger presents himself to a newspaper editor with the manuscript of a story he has written, a manuscript which causes the editor to believe it contains a terrible secret about the stranger.

As I was crossing the garden I was met by Nadia Kalenin who emerged from a shady avenue. Was it just by chance, or had she been waiting for me?

'Sergei Petrovich,' she said. I ignored her and continued walking. In an unnaturally deep voice she said, 'Stop!' The suddenness and unexpectedness of her peremptory command halted me.

'May I detain you... for a moment. You have tried to avoid me throughout the wedding luncheon. I decided to speak to you. I know that I am proud, some would say I can be egotistical, I know, and that some people find that to be overbearing, but once in a lifetime one can sacrifice pride. The question is humiliating, it is difficult for me.' Nadia looked up at me, her upper lip trembled. 'Sergei, I always think you have been separated from me by some misunderstanding, some caprice. If only I knew. I am so unhappy... all this uncertainty. I always thought I would be straightforward but... your conduct towards me is so... incomprehensible that it is impossible to arrive at a conclusion...' - I will admit that I thought her pallor was terrible - 'It is so difficult. Was I wrong to think that there was something more between us? Tell me... I was so certain that there was much more. Everything seemed possible. Everything seems to be alright until you feel that you are part of a couple. Then life becomes so much more beautiful than before and you can't believe that you were ever content with how life was before you met. And you can't go back to feeling content with how it was, how you were before. Did I misunderstand what passed between us? It is torturing me. It is so difficult to ask but please, tell me, why are you doing this?' She pressed her fingers together convulsively. Her hands were her nerves - perhaps, her spirit - restless, always moving; when, once, she had been so tranquil.

I looked away in the direction of the stable-yard, I was impatient, I wanted to be far away from the Count's estate. 'What is it that you want?' I said, again, perhaps in a harsher tome than I intended; and again she looked taken aback by my tone.

'An answer. Please.'

'To what?'

'My question is...' she looked down at her busy, nervy, *revealing* hands. She remained silent for so long that I started to move away from her. She impulsively moved after me and held my arm and whispered at last in a very quiet voice.

I could not hear what she said.

'I cannot hear you,' I said, still in the heat of the passion of the heated exchange I just had with the Count.

She tried to raise her voice, and managed to, but only slightly. This time I barely heard her.

'I do not wish to make you angry,' she whispered. 'But may I hope? Whatever the answer may be, it will be better than uncertainty. May I *hope*?'

It was surely the worst time that she could have come to me to ask such a question. I was careless. I was slightly drunk of course, and I was excited by the occurrence with Olga too, as much as the ultimatum that I had just put to the Count. My mind, in short, was elsewhere. I was more than merely careless, I was callous.

'I can't answer now!' I said, with a dismissive wave of the hand, 'I am incapable of giving any answer. It is a pity that you chose this moment to ask, when I am so distracted...'

With this, I walked away, and immediately dismissed this encounter from my mind as my mind reeled with strange sensations and thoughts brought on by the occurrences of the day. It was only later when I calmed down that I understood how stupid and cruel I had been, not to give an answer. It was such a simple and sincere question. Now, when I look back, I can scarcely believe my brutishness in brushing her away. Her simple, genuine question, that meant so much to her, but which meant, in that moment, so little to me. Yes! it is true that I was a little drunk and, yes! I was distracted but, I also know I was playing the coquette. Like a woman character in a fashionable French novel; young, lovely, and stupid; I may claim I was young, but I was certainly not lovely. If it is so difficult to understand ourselves, how are we to understand a world full of other people too?

If there is a God I plead stupidity and ignorance and ask for mercy. I would beg forgiveness, but to play the fool and ignore anothers suffering as I did ought not to be forgiven. Moreso, since I know the consequences for that proud and lovely woman I ignored. Would God, any god, forgive? God ought not to.

=

TAMBURLAINE THE GREAT by CHRISTOPHER MARLOWE, in a revised edition by James Scobie (Essential Editions), is a revision of the two part play condensed into a single play.
The volume also includes an abridged version of Marlowe's MASSACRE AT PARIS.
While these versions remain largely faithful to the original text, they have been edited throughout with some minor alterations.

> *My army, by their numbers, shall make the mountains quake,*
> *and tilt the earth; being so awed, those mountains*
> *will bow in respect, at our passage.....*

TAMBURLAINE

Is she dead? Techelles, draw your sword, and wound the earth, cleave it in two, for the world is not whole, nor I, without Zenocrate. I will descend to the infernal vaults within that fissure, and throw the Fatal Sisters into the flamed moats of hell for taking away my fair Zenocrate.

Casane and Theridamas! Arm! Raise the cannon toward the clouds, with furious shot we'll break the frame of heaven, and batter the shining palace of the sun to shiver the starry firmament and dislodge those stars. They no longer belong there!

Amorous Jove has snatched my love - meaning to place her in his high estate - making of her his queen in heaven. Whatever god holds her embraced, give him nectar, give him ambrosia. Give him what he will have, but have him give her back to me.

If it be Mars, have I not honoured war? Have I not released enough souls from their war-tortured bodies? So many as to overwhelm Hades, Elysium, Hell and Heaven?

Behold me, divine Zenocrate. Raving, desperate; goaded by
consuming furious madness! I'll break my tempered, strengthened
steel lance to burst the rusty beams of Janus' temple doors,
Let out Death and tyrannizing War, to march with me under the
blood-sodden flag; Zenocratre, look upon me, from your cloudy
throne. Pity Tamburlaine the Great, and come down from heaven
and live with me again!

THERIDAMAS
Ah, good lord. She is dead. All this raging can not make her live.
If words would serve, our shouts would rend the invisible air to
pieces. If tears would serve, our eyes would be unstoppered rivers; if
grief would serve, our murdered hearts could not hold our strained
blood. But nothing prevails against imperious, inviolate Death.
My lord. She is dead.

=

ELECTRA; INFINITE VIOLENCE by SOPHOCLES, entirely revised by
James Scobie (New Ventures in Recycled Fiction), developed from a
nineteenth century translation by Sir George Young, it expands on some of
the original themes, particularly the limit of violent revenge, hence the
sub-title, Infinite Violence.

Give me revenge, or give me destruction!

ELECTRA;
Lustrous eye that renews day to the Sky. By the blazing regalia of
your light, the splendoured greetings you send to the new coming
day, you see how many scars I have marked upon myself.
Yet your gladdening light brings no gladness to me. I always mourn
my father's loss, and am forever cheerless and sleepless; only when
exhaustless grief and sleepless exhaustion overcomes me, and frays
at my sleeplessness, that is when I can ever rest, and can forget all
troubles for a brief margin upon the lengthy page that is my life since
his slaying. Then I can only suffer a restless sleep beset with angry
dreams; always bitter, without comfort, or able to forget, being bereft
of my brother, I am the captive of a bitter family, in a bitter
household where honour has been routed to abject defeat.
It was my mother's blade that carved the treacherous blow that
struck my father's flesh with the deep lesion that insulted all
ordinary honour. A carving blow dealt as a forester cuts a high-
standing and ancient oak, backed by Aegisthus, now her bed-mate.
Together, each night, they lie in their adultery and, with it, they pile-
up a mountainous heap of ridicule upon proper form and honour.
Great light, that could not illuminate this dire deed (as the act was
closeted in a darkened room), yet I know that your bright eye must
have seen their life-destroying action.
There is no pity that flows for my father here, from any except from
myself. I cannot stop from crying or bitterest sighing, although it is
years since his slaying; still, I see it anew each day, either during the
blazing light of day or the grandeur of night's sublime moonlight
that plays, glittering, upon the sea. In the sound of the nightingale I
hear not the musical sound heard by others, but the terrified howl

and wail of Tereus (father of Itys) when Philomela and Procne killed his son, cooked him and served him as a meal.

My father was met with smiling hypocrisy by his adulterous wife, my deceiving mother; I call upon you, Ara, Goddess of Revenge and Destruction, help me requite the murder that shames his killers and his hearth. Sun, brighten the long path for my brother, to light his route back, for I, alone, can scarcely bear the burdensome weight of harrowing grief.

Throw the doors of Hades, open wide, and wedge them in gaping readiness for these murderers deaths; Ara, help me in my drowning despair! To you I plead, do not seek you to help me by saving me from this drowning in air; but give me revenge, or give me destruction!

=

THE PRIVATE MEMOIRS AND CONFESSIONS OF A JUSTIFIED SINNER by JAMES HOGG (A. Bridge & Co.), revised and edited by James Scobie. This is a revision of an early nineteenth century novel, originally published in 1824, about a number of murders, motivated by adherence to Calvinism. It is presented in the form of a memoir written by the murderer, who may - or may not (the novel is written in such a way as to, deliberately, leave the reader uncertain) - have communication with the Devil, one of the devil's helpers, or is suffering a delusion.

This edition retains the original plot - it is an entertaining and involving story - and continues to be, overwhelmingly, told in Hogg's own words, but the archaic sentence structure, language usage, and discursive form of story-telling, common at the time of publication, has been smoothed out to ease its continued enjoyment. In short, it is intended for the non-purist reader.

Set in Scotland, there is some dialogue conducted in Scots dialect, simple translations are included, again, to ease the reading experience for those who do not read or speak in Scots.

His new wife was the most severe and gloomy of all bigots to the principles of the Reformation. Hers were not the tenets of the great reformers, but theirs mightily over-strained and deformed. If theirs was an unguent hard to be swallowed; hers was that unguent embittered and overheated until the natural world could no longer bear it....

That wretch you identified, Mrs. Calvert, is the born brother of him he murdered. Sons of the same mother. But, Mrs. Calvert, that is not the main thing that so discomfited me and has shaken my nerves to pieces. Who do you think the young man was who walked in his company tonight?"

"I cannot for my life recollect, but am convinced I have seen the same fine form and face before."

"And did he seem to know us, Mrs. Calvert? and make signs to that effect?"

"He did, with great good humour."

"Mrs Calvert, hold me, else I shall fall into hysterics! Who is he? Did you note the appearance of the young gentleman you saw slain that night? Do you recollect anything of the appearance of my young master, George Colwan?"

Their looks met, and there was an unearthly amazement that gleamed from each, which, when meeting, caught real fire, and returned the flame to their heated imaginations.

"It is he, I believe," she stated, uttering the words as if inwardly. "It can be none other but he. But, no, it is impossible! I saw him stabbed; I saw him roll back in his own blood and groan away his soul. Yet, if it is not he, who can it be?" ....

...against the cant of the bigot or the hypocrite, no reasoning can avail. If you would argue until the end of life, the infallible creature must alone be right. So it proved ... one Scriptural text followed another, not in the least connected...

... "You are, Sir, a presumptuous, self-conceited pedagogue, a stirrer up of strife and commotion in church, in state, in families, and communities. You are one whose righteousness consists in splitting the doctrines of Calvin into thousands of indistinguishable slivers. In short, Sir, you are a mildew - a canker-worm in the bosom of the Reformed Church ...

..... That I was a great, a transcendent, sinner, I confess. But still, I had hopes of forgiveness, because I sinned from accident; and then I always tried to repent, and, though not always successful, I could not help that the grace of repentance was being withheld from me, I regarded myself as in no degree accountable for the failure....

I brought myself to despise, if not to abhor, the beauty of women, looking on it as the greatest snare to which mankind has ever been subjected, and though young men and maidens, and even old women (my mother among them), taxed me with being an unnatural wretch, I gloried in it...

.... "There is nothing of which I can be more certain than that the person I was was not Drummond. He could not be the killer of your much loved step-son, though he was accused of it, for he could never have doubled back upon himself in the time that elapsed, as I watched the scene unfold. We have nothing but our senses to depend upon, if these deceive us, what are we to do? I cannot account for it; nor will I ever, for it as long as I live...."

=

THE MURDER I MUST COMMIT, or, The Principle of the Extraordinary Man in History and the Application of Necessary Revolutionary Violence (A. Bridge & Co./ Essential Editions) is an extract from Fyodor Dostoyevsky's Crime and Punishment, pared down to the bare essentials of the original novel, prepared for this edition by Fforde Green and Gregory Shologanov. It concentrates solely on the essential details of the original novel, therefore it is issued under the imprint Essential Editions.

A young student believes he is compelled to commit a murder, to prove to himself that he has the same, necessary, characteristics required of a revolutionary hero, such as Napoleon once demonstrated when he took charge of the bombardment of Toulen; that such an extraordinary person has the right to commit crime for a greater good, in full knowledge that the good that arises from it justifes the crime.

"I wanted to become a new Napoleon, that is why I killed her..."

"Kill her, take her money and with it, devote oneself to the service of humanity. What do you think? Would not one tiny crime be wiped out by thousands of good deeds? For the sake of one life, thousands would be saved.... and the old woman is doing harm. She is wearing out the lives of others...."

He pulled the axe out, swung it, scarcely conscious of his own action, and almost without effort, mechanically, brought the blunt side down on her head. He seemed not to use his own strength, it was as though his hand and arms were guided. As soon as he had brought the axe down once, his strength returned.

The old woman was so short that the blow fell on the very top of her skull. She cried out, but only faintly, and sank in a heap on the floor, raising her hands to her head. Then he struck another blow, and another, each with the blunt side and on the same spot. The blood gushed as from an overfilled glass, she fell back. He stepped back, let her fall, and at once bent over her; she was dead. Her eyes seemed to be starting out of their sockets, the brow and the whole face were drawn and contorted....

"I'm done with imaginary terrors! Life is real! My life has not yet died!" he said defiantly, as though challenging some power of darkness. "I am very weak at this moment, but I... I believe my illness is over."

Pride and self-confidence continually grew stronger in him; he was becoming a different man every moment. What was it had happened to work this revolution in him? He did not know....

"In your article there was an idea that interested me, which you merely suggested without working it out entirely. There is a suggestion that there are certain persons who.... have a right to commit breaches of ordinary morality and crimes, and that the law is not for them."

Raskolnikov smiled at the exaggerated and intentional distortion of his idea by the investigating magistrate.

"A right to commit crime?" Razumihin inquired, his interest piqued by an idea new to him.

"In your article all men are divided into the 'ordinary' and the 'extraordinary.' Ordinary men have to live in submission, and have no right to transgress the law, because, obviously, they are ordinary. But extraordinary men have a right to commit any crime and to transgress the law, *because* they are extraordinary. The latter are, literally, extra ordinary, for whom no ordinary laws or morality can be framed to either limit or contain them in their ideas and actions. That was your idea, if I am not mistaken?"

"That can't be right!" Razumihin muttered, quite bewildered.

Raskolnikov smiled again. Now he knew! He saw the point at once, and knew where Porfiry Petrovitch wished to drive him, to admit the notion was his own belief; one upon which he would and could - and did - act! He decided to take up the challenge....

"Well, leaders of men, such as Solon, Mahomet, Napoleon, were all, without exception, criminals, from the very fact that, in making a new law, they transgressed the ancient law which was handed down from their ancestors and held sacred by the people, and they did not stop short at bloodshed either, if that bloodshed was of use to their cause, and which was often of innocent persons fighting bravely in defence of the ancient law....

"What's to be done?" Sonia asked, now weeping hysterically.

"What's to be done? Break what must be broken, once and for all, and take the suffering on oneself. You don't understand? Yet you read the Bible, you know of the suffering of Christ. Christ took on the suffering of all humanity that was to follow him! Life breaks us, those of us who cannot accept the indifferent universe, and..." he paused. "You'll understand later.... Freedom and power, and above all, the Power! Over all creation and this entire ant-heap!... That is the goal, remember! That's my farewell message. Perhaps it's the last time I shall speak to you. If I don't come to-morrow, you'll hear of it - then you will know why I speak the words I do - and will remember these words. And some day, in years to come, you'll understand what they meant... Good-bye...."

Raskolnikov was sitting with compressed lips, his feverish eyes fixed on Porfiry Petrovitch.

"In the general case, the case for which all legal forms and rules are intended, such cases rarely exist at all, for every crime, as soon as it occurs, at once becomes a special case, and sometimes it may be a case unlike any that's gone before.

"If I leave a man alone, if I don't touch him and don't worry him, but let him know or suspect that I know all and am watching him day and night, and if he is in continual suspicion, and terrified of the suspicion, he'll be bound to lose his head. He'll come to me, of himself, or maybe do something which will make it so plain, it's delightful. It may be so with a simple peasant, but with an intelligent cultivated man it's a dead certainty.

"Then, there are nerves, you cannot overlook them! They become sick, nervous and irritable!... then how they suffer! That is a regular gold-mine for us. That is what does half our work for us! It's no anxiety to me if he is running about the town free! Let him! Let him walk about.... I know well enough that I've caught him...."

Raskolnikov made no reply; he sat pale, gazing with intensity into Porfiry's face.

"This is beyond the cat playing with a mouse. He can't be showing off his power with no motive..." he thought. "He is too clever for that... You are pretending you know more than you do, in order to scare me! You've no evidence, You want to make me lose my head, to work me up and to crush me. But why give me the hint? Is he reckoning on my shattered nerves? ..."

"Since you have taken such a step, you must... fulfil the demands of justice. First, there is God, second, there is morality, third, there are our human laws, and forth, there is personal conscience; each who kills will be judged by at least one of these, haven't you discovered that it is the forth of these that is your judge? And a harsh and austere judge too. This is why you are fevered, and faint, and rage, and am forgetful, and weep...."

"When do you mean to arrest me?"

"Well, I can't let you walk at liberty for more than another day or two. Think it over... pray to God. It's in your interest."

"And what if I run?" asked Raskolnikov with a strange smile, the smile of someone who still wishes to escape, but knows they will not; as a rabbit in a snare wishes to escape, yet, being caught in the snare, they cannot.

"No, you won't do that. A peasant would run, a dissenter or one of our present day revolutionaries, they would run, for they are only the follower of another man's ideals, people such as them, they will believe in anything, and, without God, they must believe in something! But you've ceased to believe in your theory already..."

.... "All men shed blood, it has always flowed in streams, and for this, men are often crowned, and feted as benefactors of all mankind. They cause the deaths of thousands, and they are lauded, I kill one useless old woman, who was near death anyway, and it is *I* that is the criminal! I, too, wanted to do good and would have done hundreds, if not thousands, of good deeds too..."

He thought of his mother and beloved sister, thought of how they would learn of his actions, his crime. He pictured himself as he had been when he had set off for the university from that dusty town on the sun-baked steppe; when he had been dressed in a new suit with new boots, with a small suitcase of clothes, and text books, and with a copy of Pushkin's Eugene Onegin, and the Theban trilogy; he pictured himself as he was when he said farewell to his kin; he saw the large tears that had flowed down his sister's face, felt the grip of his mother and his sister's arms as they had flung them around his neck before he stepped into the railway carriage. "I am the hope of the family!" he thought as he felt overwhelming contempt for himself, of how he had let them down....

=

A HERO OF OUR TIME by MICHEAL LERMANTOV (A. Bridge & Co./ Essential Editions) edited by Gregory Shologanov.
A lightly abridged version of Lermantov's fictional memoir, this version eschews much of the discursive form of story telling of the period and concentrates solely on the essential details of the original novel, hence this version is issued under the imprint, Essential Editions.

The diary of a young officer, who had been posted to the Caucasus Mountains during the early nineteenth century, tells of his thoughts and impressions of life; he is what nowadays would be termed an existenialist. He wins the love of a daughter of a Muslim tribal leader, discards her, seduces a young Princess while renewing an old love affair, he also renews an old antipathy with a fellow soldier, with whom he fights and survives a dual.

Secret grief is killing her...

We, the miserable descendants of those wise people of former times, roam the earth, without faith, without pride, and without terror - except that involuntary awe which makes the heart shrink at the thought of our inevitable end - we are no longer capable of great sacrifices, either for the good of mankind or even for our own happiness, because we know the impossibility of such happiness; and, just as our ancestors used to fling themselves from one delusion to another, we pass indifferently from doubt to doubt, without possessing, as they did, any hope at all....

I have passed that period of spiritual life when happiness alone is sought, when the heart feels the urgent necessity of violently and passionately loving somebody. Now my only wish is to be loved, and by very few. I even think that I would be content with one constant attachment. A wretched habit! ...

He once told me that he would rather do a favour for an enemy than for a friend, because, in the latter case, it would mean selling his beneficence, whilst hatred only increases proportionately to the magnanimity of the adversary!

Women have been known to fall madly in love with men of the sort, and have no desire to exchange their ugliness for beauty. We must give women their due: they possess an instinct for spiritual beauty, for which reason, possibly, men such as he love women so passionately...

Our conversation commenced with slander; I passed on to review our present and absent acquaintances; at first I exposed their ridiculous, and then their bad, sides. I began in jest, and ended in genuine malice. At first she was amused, but afterwards she became frightened.

"You are a dangerous man!" Princess Mary said. "I would rather perish in the woods under the knife of an assassin than under your tongue...

I love my enemies, though not in the Christian sense. They amuse me, they stir my blood.... I sometimes despise myself. Is not that the reason why I despise others also? I have grown incapable of noble impulses.

In my place, another would have offered Princess Mary *son coeur et sa fortune;* but, for me, the word "marry" has a kind of magical power. However passionately I love a woman, if she only gives me to feel that I have to marry her - then farewell, my love! My heart turns to stone, and nothing will warm it anew....

Secret grief is killing her; she will not confess it, but I am convinced that you are the cause: you think, perhaps, that I am looking for rank or immense wealth - my daughter's happiness is my sole desire....

If I am to be killed in the dual then the loss to the world will not be great; and I am downright weary of everything. My whole life I live again in memory, and, involuntarily, I ask myself: 'why have I lived? - for what purpose was I born?' A purpose there must have been, and, surely, mine was an exalted destiny, because I feel that within my soul are immeasurable powers. But, because I was not able to discover that destiny, I have allowed myself to be carried away by the allurements of passions, inane and ignoble though they have proved...

To no one has the receipt of my love brought happiness, because I have never sacrificed anything for the sake of those I have loved: for myself alone I have loved - only for my own pleasure. I have only satisfied the cravings of my heart, greedily draining their feelings, their tenderness, their joys, their sufferings - and I have never been able to sate myself...

Grushnitski placed himself opposite me and, at a given signal, began to raise his pistol. I noticed how he shook. He aimed at my forehead. Fury began to seethe within me....

You will say that the cause of morality gains nothing by this book. I beg your pardon. People have been surfeited with sweetmeats and their digestion has been ruined: bitter medicines, sharp truths, are necessary.....

=

ANNA KARENINA by LEO TOLSTOI (A. Bridge & Co./ Essential Editions) an abridgement by Belle Ellis and Gregory Shologanov of Tolstoi's classic novel set in 1870's Russia. This version concentrates entirely on the story of Anna Karenina, Karenin, and Vronsky; the other strands of the original novel have been almost entirely excised, except where the story of other characters overlap with that of the three main characters. As a consequence, in a paperback edition, Anna Karenina does not feature in the story until, usually, around a hundred pages into the story, in this version she appears almost immediately, when she is met by her brother at the railway station and is introduced to Vronsky.

For Vronsky, that which had been - for almost a whole year - the one absorbing desire of his life, the one which had replaced all his old desires; and that which, for Anna, had been an impossible, terrible - and for that reason - more entrancing dream of bliss, that desire had been fulfilled. He stood before her, pale.

She felt so sinful, and, as now there was no one in her life but him, to him she addressed her prayer for forgiveness. Looking at him, she had a physical sense of her humiliation, and she could say nothing more. He felt what a murderer must feel, when he sees the body. And that body, robbed by him of life, was their love, the first stage of their love. There was something awful and revolting in the memory of what had been bought at this fearful price of shame. Shame at their spiritual nakedness crushed her and infected him.

Vronsky covered her face and shoulders with kisses. She held his hand and did not stir. Yes! These kisses - it was these kisses that has brought this shame. Yes, and one hand, which will always be mine - the hand of my accomplice. She lifted up that hand and kissed it. He sank on his knees and tried to see her face; but she hid it, and said nothing. At last, as though making an effort over herself, she got up and pushed him away. Her face was still as beautiful, but it was only the more pitiful for that.

"All is over," she said; "I have nothing but you. Remember that."

"I can never forget what is my whole life. For one moment of bliss..."

"Happiness? Bliss?" she said. She rose quickly and moved away from him. "Not a word more," she said, and with a look of chill despair, incomprehensible to him, she parted from him.

She felt that at that moment she could not put into words the sense of shame, of rapture, and of horror at this stepping into a new life, and she did not want to speak of it, to vulgarise this feeling by mere words. But later too, and the next day and the third day, she still found no words in which she could express the complexity of her feelings; indeed, she could not even find thoughts in which she could clearly think out all that was in her soul.

She said to herself: 'Just now I can't think of it, later on, when I am calmer.' But this calm period for thought never came. 'Not now. Later, later,' she said, 'when I am calmer,' she repeated over and over.

But in dreams, when she had no control over her thoughts, her position presented itself to her in all its hideous nakedness. One dream often haunted her. She dreamed that both were her husbands at once, that both were lavishing caresses on her. Her husband was there, he was weeping, kissing her hands, and saying, "How happy we are now! And how beautiful it is now!" And Alexey Vronsky was there too, and he too was her husband. She was marvelling that it had once seemed impossible to her, and she was explaining to them, laughing, how much simpler this was, and that now both of them were happy and contented. But this dream always weighed upon her and woke her.

=

THE MAID OF ORLEAN by FREDERICH SCHILLER, and COMPELLED BY VISIONS by JAMES SCOBIE (A. Bridge & Co./New Ventures in Recycled Fiction) is, in the case of Maid of Orlean, a lightly abridged version of Schiller's play, Compelled by Visions is the first play in the volume, and is a reworking of Schiller's play.

COMPLELLED BY VISIONS;
DUNOIS
Is her father in English pay? He must be. This is no ordinary accusation, it is denunciation.

DUCHATEL
But if it were so...?

DUNOIS
I do not believe it!

SOREL

She is struck dumb by her father's treacherous tongue!

THIBAUT
Before that awful name which is feared everywhere, even in the deep
of Hell, she must be silent! Was she commissioned by God to be a
Holy one? It was conceived on a cursed spot beneath the Druid tree.
It was there that she bartered away her immortal soul. Why did she
do this? An ordinary life as a shepherd held no appeal. She sought a
transient, worldly glory. Have you never asked how else could a
woman overcome armies of men? Let her bare her arm, and you will
see the impression of the fatal marks made there by demons!

DUNOIS
There are no such marks! I have seen nothing but the slash mark of a
blade!

BURGUNDY
This is too horrible! Yet we must believe a father's words. Who
would give such trenchant evidence against his own daughter .

DUNOIS
Why must we believe a father's words? What does he offer but
accusations. He brings shame upon himself. Did she not persuade
you, Burgundy, to come to a state of peace and reconciliation? Where
is the Devil-work in that?

SOREL [Dashes forward to JOHANNA]
Speak, Maiden! This is a fatal silence! We trust in you! We believe
you! Annihilate this horrifying accusation. One word shall be
sufficient. Speak! Declare your innocence, and we will believe you.

[JOHANNA remains motionless; AGNES SOREL steps back in
horror]

DUNOIS
What Agnes Sorel says is true, 'break this spell'. That is truth. Her
father is involved in some Devil practice, he has cast a spell on her,
that is why she stands rigid and speechless.

LA HIRE
She is frightened, that is all. It is horror and astonishment at the
crazed accusation. She cannot speak. Who could do otherwise before
such a charge? Even holy innocence must tremble.
[He approaches her]
Collect yourself, Johanna! Your innocence is transcendent, it is a
lightning flash that strikes such slander to the earth! Punish this
doubt with your noble wrath , it is an insult to your high and Holy
state.

[JOHANNA remains motionless and silent]

DUNOIS

Why do the people fear and princes tremble? We have rushed the enemy, we have been defeated many times before our recent victories, yet we faced those dangers time and again. But now you tremble? Look! It is a woman, a Maid.

I'll stake all my noble blood, my honour and battle valour, on her innocence! Here, I throw out the challenge. Who will venture to maintain her guilt? Regard this, could it be that Thiabalt, her father, like the Burgundians once were, is in English pay, to bring this foul accusation?

[Some in the crowd seem to be persuaded by this but before he can say more there is a loud clap of thunder; all are horror-struck]

THIBAUT
Answer me! By Him whose thunder rolls above! Declare the lie and proclaim your innocence. Say that the enemy of man does not have hold on your heart!
[Another clap of thunder, louder than the first; the people flee on all sides]
- The over-world, above the skies, answers for you! In those thunder rolls! It declares against you! It declares that you are the enemy of man!

BURGUNDY
These signs appal!
[To the KING]
- My king! Forsake this fearful place!

DUCHATEL
No royal could... no mortal can, stand in the presence of such a contaminating presence.

=

TO BE A PILGRIM; Being the Private Memoirs and Confessions of a Justified Sinner by AMES COTT, (New Ventures in Recycled Fiction) is a reworking of James Hogg's novel (see above) into the form of a modern day piece of investigative journalism, or history writing, attempting to discover the truth of past events, that fascinate for their own sake, and drawing upon family history, journals, letters, and local legends; it includes the 'confession' as used in the original novel, has some excisions, but is also supplemented with further scenes that do not occur in the original book.

   This strange bird-like creature arrived above my head and wheeled about several times, the body and face altering as he circled. It's wings began to dissolve and as he descended ever lower, they became the robes of a minister of the church. Upon touching the ground I saw that, instantly, it's body was becoming ever more shrunken and mis-shapen and his face blacken and shrivel as though he had been burnt to cinders, possibly even, burnt alive. Gil-Martin had become a figure, scarcely human at all, of a disgusting disfigurement.

Yet, when he spoke, he maintained a tone of supercilious condescension even as he complained of the way that I, Robert Wringham, his servant, his earthly agent for his great works, had not met all the promise that I had shown when he had first appeared to me, that blessed day when I had first been confirmed in the 'justification' of the Elect. He complained of how I, who had followed his ministrations with so little quail, had always vacillated at crucial moments. He harangued me with an endless list of 'what-might-have-beens', if I had ever been a person worthy of Gil-Martin's advice, attention and trust.

Through all this his voice was a cankering cawing sound, fully like the sound of a forest full of rooks or ravens. He hardly spoke in English, or in words at all. Yet the import and intent of his constant careening catalogue of faults and accusations were as clear to me as though he were speaking with the clearest diction.

He admitted no role or responsibility in both our downfalls. In his own fervent and wanton plunge into the frauds and deceit of his appearance, of his taking on my own appearance around Dalcastle. I now knew! It played on my mind in the form of some curious vaporous half-forgotten memory. Yet, knowing this, I did not have the will to raise the matter, either as observation, as complaint, or as accusation; the subduction of the former laird into the body of Gil-Martin and HIS will, was so complete. It had been his intoxicating of me, and his binding of myself up in my own mind - so that I did know of the ordinary passages of the seasons, and of time, when I had become the new laird - that led to all these troubles now. Yes; what I might have been, and what we might have been, but for this plunge into the sin of all sensualists. How he had taken over my body to indulge himself, always taking the guise of the new laird, that is, when he wasn't 'haunting' the estate in the form and guise of my murdered half-brother. It was this diversion into ruinous sensuousness, of seduction, of defilement, of excess, that had wreaked our high, and great, and fine, and exquisite, and astonishing designs, rather than convert them, with diligence, into accomplished feats.

There, by the bridge over the wee burn in the Border country, I finally, through the mangled and shredded remains of the slight connection I still held to humanity, was fully bereft of hope.

From fleeting changes in his visage, Gil-Martin's face became like a whirlpool, a seething tumult, of all his changing selves. His ravaged, wreaked body now reeked of all that was rotten and rotting. Decay dominated his demeanour, his figure, his stature.

"Look at me, look what you have done to me! All the world was yours."

=

I STAND ACCUSED by FfORDE GREEN (New Ventures in Recycled Fiction) is a reworking of the novel, Innocence / Guilt (see above). It is the same story in every detail, except the location of the story has been removed from southern Russia to the north of England, to Yorkshire, and includes incidental details of parts of Leeds, West Yorkshire and North Yorkshire. It is published for the sole purpose of satisfying the interest of those who would not read a story *because* it is set in Russia, but will enjoy a story with local details.

An affable stranger presents himself to a newspaper editor with the manuscript of a story, a manuscript which causes the editor to believe it contains a terrible secret about the stranger.

"I discovered the terrible secret of a terrible man..."

Love and murder, I thought, as he had admitted it was hardly original and it was difficult to see that there would be anything new that he would be able to add to that worn-out theme. I closed it, but rather than get out of my seat to put it on the stack in the cupboard I slipped it away in a desk drawer. There it remained for several weeks. But one day as I was leaving the office for a long weekend in North Yorkshire, at a hotel on the moors, I took it with me as something to read.

When I was seated in the railway coach I opened it. I always have difficulty starting reading a story, as the author is establishing the basis of the story and the 'voice' that they will use in the telling, so I began to read from the middle. It was quite short so I had finished it by the time the train arrived at Pickering. I put the manuscript away and was driven, with other passengers, from the station to the hotel in a carriage; it was late evening, a sweet spring evening, with warm intimations of summer and I wished to enjoy the evening air. All the while though, there was something in the story that was stirring in my mind.

Later, after I had met my wife and two daughters, after I had unpacked, and we had eaten our evening meal, I returned to the MS, and I turned back to the beginning and read the whole story through again. That night I read the entire story through. I had ordered two bottles of wine to be brought to our room, but had opened neither. When I finished reading the story for the third time I drank the bottle of red wine and reflected upon the story. Then I returned to the story and read through selected passages. By the time I finished the sun was rising, it was mid-summer, and I was pacing the balcony rubbing my temples as if I were attempting to rub out of my mind some new, painful and unwanted thoughts that had seated themselves there. It appeared to me that I had discovered, or had revealed to me - by the story itself - the terrible secret of a terrible man. This is the story that left me in this agitated state....

=

STORIES FROM THE STREETS OF ST PETERSBURG, 1868 (New Ventures in Recycled Fiction/ FictionFaction). An extract from Fyodor Dostoyevsky's Crime and Punishment, prepared for this edition by Fforde Green and Gregory Shologanov. It reworks elements of the novel into a series of short stories telling tales, drawn from life, set in the streets and boarding-houses of a working class district of Petersburg during the hot summer of a year in the middle of the nineteenth century, although, in many of the details, they are stories that could be told, with few alterations, of many large city anywhere in the world, today - so little changes.

The young man recognised the wife at once. She was rather tall, slim and graceful, terribly emaciated, with a hectic flush on her cheeks. She was pacing around the little room; her breathing came in broken gasps. Her eyes glittered, as in a fever, and she looked around with a harsh stare. She seemed to be about thirty years old... She was lost in thought. The room was close, she had not opened the window.

The youngest child, a girl of six, was asleep, sitting curled up on the floor with her head leaning on the sofa. A younger boy stood wailing in the corner, probably he had just had a beating from his mother. Beside him stood a girl of nine years, tall and thin, wearing a ragged chemise with an ancient cashmere shawl flung over her bare shoulders. Her thin arm was round her brother's neck while she whispered something, trying to comfort him. Her large dark eyes looked larger still from the thinness of her frightened face, and were watching her mother warily.

The drunk man, leaning on the young man, did not enter, but dropped on his knees. The woman, seeing a stranger, walked toward the door to close it and uttered a scream on seeing her husband, drunk again, in the doorway.

"He has come back! though it is better that he had not. We might have finally been rid of him! It is he who takes food from the mouths of children! What's in your pockets, show me! Where is the money!"

As he struggled to his feet she started to search him. The drunk man submissively and obediently held up both arms to ease the search. Not a kopeck was found....

In the heat of mid-afternoon, on an almost deserted boulevard, the girl seemed hardly to know what she was doing; she crossed one leg over the other, lifting it indecorously, so that he saw her stockings were not tied up, and she showed every sign of not even knowing she was in a public place. She was completely drunk. It was a shocking sight....

The young student took the policeman by the arm and drew him towards her.

"Look, this girl is hopelessly drunk, she has just come down the boulevard. There is no telling what has happened, and who has done this to her, she does not look like a professional. It's more likely she has been given drink somewhere and... and they've put her out into the street like this. Look at the way her dress has been put on: she has not dressed herself... even the professionals attempt to make themselves presentable... she has been dressed by unpractised hands, a man's hands. See how it is torn too. Now, *he*, too, has seen her, drunk, and is eager to get hold of her, to get her away somewhere while she is in this state. I saw him watching her and following her, but I prevented him..."

The policeman saw it all in a moment. He turned to consider the girl and bent to examine her more closely; his face worked with genuine compassion....

Timidly a young woman made her way through the crowd, her appearance was strange in the midst of the poverty, ragged clothes, illness and death. She, too, was dressed in scarcely little better than rags, material of the cheapest sort, but it was gutter finery, and it unmistakably betrayed its purpose. The young woman, Sophia, stopped and looked around her, bewildered. She forgot her clothing, the gaudy fourth-hand silk dress, with its ridiculous long train, her immense crinoline that filled up the doorway, and her light-coloured slipper shoes, and the parasol she carried, the absurd partly-crushed and misshapen round straw hat with its flaring flame-coloured feather. Under the rakishly-tilted hat was a pale face. She was a small thin girl of eighteen, or less, rather pretty, with wonderful large blue eyes and with fine fair hair. Her eyes, widened by fright, seemed to be larger for sitting in such a small face. She was out of breath with running. She looked down at the figure on the sofa, that of her crushed and dying father...

On the canal bank there was a crowd of gutter children. The hoarse broken voice of the mother was heard as they approached, still at a distance, it wailed rather than sang; it was a strange spectacle that had to attract a street crowd.

The mother was in her old striped dress, she was wearing a torn straw hat, crushed on one side; she was frantic, exhausted and breathless. Her wasted face looked more suffering than ever, and suddenly much more aged. She coaxed the children, more by shouting at them than by encouragement, told them, in front of the crowd, how to dance and what to sing, and in her desperation, she hit them... If she noticed any decently dressed person passing by, she appealed to them to see what her children "from a genteel, one may say aristocratic, house" had been brought to. If she heard jeering in the crowd, she would begin squabbling with them. Some laughed, others shook their heads, but everyone was curious and could not help but stare at the sight of the woman with the frightened, weeping children.

She clapped her wasted hands, and made her youngest two children dance and have Polly sing. She joined in the singing too, but would break down with a fearful cough. A little effort had been made to dress the children in street singers outfits. The boy had a turban made of red and white cut-off's to look like a Turkman. There had been no costume for Lily other than her mother's discarded black material folded over, and worn like a peasant skirt or apron, along with a red cap, or rather the night cap that had belonged to her husband, rolled up and decorated with the broken half of an ostrich feather, which was the final rememberance that the mother had in her possession of her young, happy, dancing days. The eldest child, Polly, was in her everyday dress; she looked in timid perplexity at her mother, all the while she struggled to not show the tears which seemed ready to be shaken loose upon her trembling fearful face. She dimly realised her mother's condition....

The fact is he never expected such an ending to the affair, he never dreamed that two destitute and defenceless women could escape his control. This idea was strengthened by his own vanity. He had made his way up from nothing, and was inclined toward self-admiration, and he had the highest opinion of his intelligence. What he valued above all else was the money he had amassed by his labour: for it was through his money that he had made himself the equal of those who had been his superiors.

When he had reminded the young woman he intended to marry that he had decided to take her in spite of the bad reputation that had become attached to her, he had done so with perfect sincerity. And yet, when he made his offer, he knew of the groundlessness of the gossip, which was by then disbelieved by all the townspeople, who now spoke in her defence.

He still thought highly of his proposal and regarded himself as something heroic. In speaking of it he did so with the feelings of a benefactor who was about to reap the fruits of his good deeds and to hear agreeable flattery....

She drew a revolver from her pocket, and cocked it.

"A-ha! So that's it!" he declared, surprised. "That alters the affair. You've made things wonderfully clear. But that revolver is mine. And how I've searched for it!"

"It's not your revolver, it belonged to your wife! *You* were a bankrupt when she married you. There was nothing of yours in *her* house. I took it when I began to suspect what you're capable of. If you advance a single step, I'll kill you.... I hated you always, always..."

"I know you will shoot, you pretty, lovely, wild creature. So be it! Shoot! Perhaps I do not wish to live any longer...."

An expression of puzzlement flashed across the young woman's face, through the anger. Deathly pale now, she stared at him, measuring the distance and awaiting his move. Her big, dark eyes flashed fiercely. He had never seen her so beautiful, the fire glowing in her eyes as she positioned the revolver seemed to kindle a deep anguish in him. He wished to be by her side, he forgot the pistol, and her warning, for a moment, and took a step forward. She fired. The bullet grazed his head, by the hairline. He stopped, looked around at where the bullet buried itself in the wall plaster and laughed softly....

They stared at each other without speaking. It struck the man as irregular for any man to stand staring and not saying a word.

"What do you want?" the gatekeeper demanded.

"Nothing, brother, good morning," answered the man. "I am leaving for foreign parts today. America," the man said as he took out the revolver. He checked the charge and cocked it. "Perhaps the charge is so damp," he thought, "from sitting in my wet overcoat through all the past evening and night. It might misfire. That would hardly be a blessing, but I would just have to go back into town and buy the necessaries. A temporary postponement. Would I reconsider? No! I've considered the matter enough, I am decided."

The other man raised his eyebrows, looked about him at the deserted early morning street, wondering why a stranger should take out a gun and wish to shoot *him*.

"What is it you want?" he exclaimed.

"This? Do not concern yourself," the other man assured him. "Well, brother, good morning. When you are asked, just say the man said he was going to the New World. Good-bye."

Later, when he was being questioned, the man in the soldier's great coat, the gate-keeper, told of how the other man gripped the revolver so firmly that his knuckles were white, how he lifted it to his right temple, while he looked at the gate-keeper. "God in heaven!" he exclaimed to the examiner, "why did he come to stand in front of me?" The gate-keeper told how the man had then turned his head away, he seemed to do this so his blood would not splash the gate-keeper.

He pulled the trigger. The pistol did not misfire....

=

Printed in Great Britain
by Amazon